Amy Cross is the author of more than 200 horror,
paranormal, fantasy and thriller novels.

1800

THE HAUNTING OF HADLOW HOUSE BOOK FOUR

AMY CROSS

This edition
first published by Blackwych Books Ltd
United Kingdom, 2023

Also available in e-book format.

www.blackwychbooks.com

CONTENTS

1800

PROLOGUE

February 1800...

A COLD WIND BLEW snow through the forest as two men pushed onward, dragging their sacks of plundered goods. Having been out poaching for several hours now, Charles Evans and his son Nicholas were ready to get home and warm their hands by the fire. First, though, they needed to navigate the treacherous snowbanks that had built up between the trees.

"Let's hope nobody's out following footprints tonight," Nicholas muttered, shivering slightly as the collar of his jacket flapped in the wind. "We'd be easy enough to find if -"

"Wait!" Charles said, stopping suddenly and

holding up a hand to silence his son.

"What is it?"

"Have we made a mistake?" Charles whispered, watching the darkness ahead as he tried to make sense of the forest beyond the falling snow. "I was careful, but..."

His voice trailed off.

"What is it?" Nicholas asked again, struggling to take a step forward before stopping again as he realized that he could just about see a shape somewhere up ahead, some kind of dark facade looming from the gloom. "I thought we were taking the southern path back home? Why's there a house here?"

"That's not just any house," Charles told him. "That's Hadlow House."

"Hadlow... I've heard of that before. Isn't that -"

"No-one has any business going anywhere near that place," Charles said firmly, and now his voice was gripped tight in the vice of fear. "It's been twenty-five years since any soul ventured even as close as we are now. This snow must have momentarily robbed me of my senses and led me astray. If we're within sight of Hadlow House, we must have veered too far to the north."

He turned and began to push on in a

different direction.

"Come on," he said, sounding a little out of breath now. "We'll have to go around."

"But it's cold," Nicholas complained, still watching the house. "Couldn't we just break the rules this once?"

Charles stopped and turned to him.

"It's just a house," Nicholas pointed out with a shrug. "We've never been superstitious people, have we? So why start now?"

"You don't know what you're talking about," Charles replied. "You're only a young 'un, I bet you don't even remember the trouble that occurred out at that place."

"All I know is that people tend to go quiet whenever Hadlow House is mentioned," Nicholas told him. "I know there are supposed to be all these terrible tales associated with the place, but I always assumed that those tales were nothing more than gossip, spread by weak-minded women such as... well, such as mother, to be honest."

"Ordinarily I'd agree with you," Charles said, "but when it comes to Hadlow House things are a little different." He turned and looked between the trees again, and once more he saw the faintest dark smudge of the house's outline in the distance. "I remember the day well when men from our village went out to that house and apprehended an American who was plotting against the king. Some good friends died in the service of our country, and I have no doubt that the house itself played some villainous role in the events. Or if not the house, then some dark spirits that lurk within."

"Now you sound like Mother," Nicholas suggested with a faint, nervous smile. "I know women tend to have these feelings, but I never expected such foolishness from you, Father."

"There's a fair amount of land attached to the house," Charles explained, "and I'm no more likely to set foot on the land than I am to approach the house itself. You might not like it, my boy, but I'm afraid we're going to have to go all the way around the edge of the property."

"But that'll take -"

"And there'll be no arguing about it," Charles added. "Not this time. I'm older and wiser than you, and you're just going to listen to my advice. Is that clear?"

"Absolutely," Nicholas replied, even though he felt that his curiosity had been piqued. "I suppose you'd better lead the way, then. I know better than to argue with you, Father, even if I have to admit that part of me wants to march right up to that house and prove that there's nothing nefarious going on." He began to follow Charles through the snow, as they skirted the perimeter of Hadlow House's land on their way back to Cobblefield. "This is all just a lot of fuss over nothing, if you ask me," he added. "Shouldn't we have moved beyond this childish nonsense by now? Anyone with half a brain knows that there's no such things as ghosts or spirits or things that go bump in the night."

As they walked away, the sound of their footsteps became fainter and fainter. For a few minute they could still be heard arguing as their feet crunched through the snow, but finally the forest fell still again, save for the gentle rustling of more snow drifting down and landing on the steps that had come before. This part of the forest had long since been abandoned by most of the wildlife, and even the trees had been looking weak and sickly for a while before the snap of cold weather had arrived. A few hundred meters away, a wall marked the edge of Hadlow House's land, and a few hundred meters beyond that stood the house itself, dark and icy cold in the night air. Thick snow blanketed the ground, proving that nobody had gone near the house in quite some time; indeed, nobody had gone near the place since an awful night of death and tragedy twenty-five years earlier.

At one of the downstairs windows, the

faintest hint of a woman's figure could be seen staring out from behind the dirty and scratched glass.

Still waiting.

CHAPTER ONE

STANDING IN THE KITCHEN at Cobblefield
Stables, Anne Smudge stared down at the dirty pots
in the sink and found herself wondering why she'd
ever got married in the first place.

She could hear her husband Horace
stumbling around drunk in the storeroom. Ten years
earlier Horace Smudge had seemed like a decent,
dependable man who could be relied upon to take
over the Purkiss family business; he'd presented
himself as a man of vision, a man of character, and
certainly not as a man who liked to drink three pints
of ale for breakfast. Gradually, over time, the facade
had fallen, to the extent that Anne now found
herself contemplating the thought that she'd have
been better off remaining unmarried. There were

plenty of young men from the village to employ for the hard physical work, and she felt sure that her understanding of the business side of things was equal to whatever vague thoughts drifted through her husband's head. Then again, she knew that if she hadn't married Horace, then she would never have welcomed into her life the one person who made all the hardship worthwhile.

"Mother," Charlotte said from the doorway, "can I go out and play with Molly?"

Turning, Anne saw her nine-year-old daughter watching with a smile already on her face. Anne remembered herself at that age, but she felt that Charlotte possessed more energy and curiosity than almost anyone else she'd ever encountered. And then, before she could reply to her daughter and tell her that there was no point going out in the snow, they both heard a loud crashing sound coming from the storeroom.

"It's alright!" Horace called out drunkenly. "I just knocked some things over, that's all! No need to worry!"

"You don't want to play with me?" Anne asked, heading over to the table and moving another chess piece. "You'll only understand the rules properly if you actually keep at the game."

"We'll only play in the street," Charlotte

continued, having long since learned – even at her tender age – to simply ignore her father whenever he was in such a terrible state. "We won't leave the village, I promise."

"And why would you even want to go out in the cold?" Anne asked, realizing that chess was of no interest to her daughter.

"It's something to do," Charlotte replied. "Molly's mother lets her go out."

"You mustn't stray too far," Anne told her. "I want to be able to see you whenever I come to the edge of the yard and look out. Is that understood?"

"Of course."

"And if -"

Before Anne could get another word out, they both heard a heavy thud coming from the room directly above. They both looked up at the ceiling, and then – when Anne glanced at her daughter again – she saw the fear in the little girl's eyes. In that moment Anne understood something that she had perhaps been trying to ignore for a while now, which was the fact that on certain days it was not Horace at all who caused the most disturbance in the house, and that Anne was quite right to want to get away for a few hours.

"Wrap up warm," Anne said firmly. "I don't want you catching a cold."

"I won't," Charlotte replied, already turning and hurrying toward the front door, clearly desperate to go and join her friend.

Anne stood for a moment and listened to the sound of Horace struggling to tidy up in the storeroom. That din was troublesome enough, but at least it was mostly harmless. In truth, she was more concerned about the other sound she could hear; looking at the ceiling again, she heard the faintest creaking of a floorboard in one of the bedrooms, and she let out a sigh as she realized that she was going to have to go and check on her grandmother.

Well, not her grandmother, exactly. But that was how she always thought of the woman.

***

"Patience?" Anne said softly once she'd pushed open the bedroom door. "Is everything alright up here?"

She looked into the gloomy room and tried to ignore the stale fusty smell that filled the air. Listening for a few seconds, she heard nothing at all to suggest that there was a problem, although she could already see that the bedclothes had been cast aside from the bed and left to hang down, with the tail of one of the sheets dangling into the metal bedpan that stood next to one of the wooden legs. Anne felt a glimmer of frustration – she'd told Patience to be careful of soiling the sheets in such a manner – but she also knew that frustration was pointless. After all, at such an advanced age, Patience was far beyond the point of understanding such things.

Hearing a shuffling sound, Anne turned and looked into the corner of the room, and she saw that Patience – her ninety-nine-year-old frame dressed in nothing more than a thin nightgown – was looking through some old boxes on one of the dressers.

"Now, what are you doing out of bed?" Anne asked, opting to sound as friendly and cheery as possible as she marched across the room and pulled the curtains open. "Don't you remember that we've talked about this before? You're only going to fall again and hurt yourself. Do you remember when you broke your arm?"

Turning to look across the room, which was now flooded with light, she felt a shudder pass through her chest as she saw Patience staring back at her. She remembered how Patience had been so strong and sturdy many years earlier, but now her almost blind white eyes glared out from a lined face; her expression was one of shock, with perhaps a little confusion added, and thin white hair hung down from a few remaining patches on her scalp. As she watched Patience for a few seconds, Anne felt a rush of sympathy and love for the woman with whom she'd quarreled so many times when they were both younger, and she knew that the mind in that head was barely even the real Patience.

Had the real Patience ever truly recovered from the loss of Daniel twenty-five years earlier?

"What are you doing there?" Anne asked, taking a step forward.

Patience murmured something unintelligible before turning back to the boxes.

"Can I help?" Anne asked, advancing across the room while trying to see what Patience's thin, liver-spotted hands were doing in one of the boxes. "You know you shouldn't be out of bed like this."

Again Patience spoke, or at least she *tried* to speak; whether she actually expected her words to be heard was another matter entirely, for she seemed most of the time to exist entirely in her own little world.

"Is that some of your old jewelry?" Anne asked as she stopped next to her and looked into one of the boxes. She saw a few necklaces and brooches. "Some of those belonged to Great Grandmother Rose, didn't they?" she continued. "And some to my own mother?"

She waited, wondering how Patience would react to this mention of the past. Sometimes names such as Daniel and Rose and Anne seemed to comfort her, but at other times she seemed almost horrified by any mention of the old days. Anne knew that Patience had been born and raised in London, and that she had moved to Cobblefield with her own parents, to live at Hadlow House. She paused, but she knew that there was no point contemplating any of the other events that had happened so very many years ago, and then – before she had to worry about what she might say next – one of the necklaces slithered out of Patience's shaking hands and fell to the floor.

"Let me get that," Anne said, crouching down and picking the necklace up, before getting back to her feet and handing it to Patience again. "If -"

"Has anybody gone there?" Patience asked suddenly, her voice sounding cracked and dry.

"I don't -"

"Has anybody gone to that house?" Patience snapped.

"No," Anne replied, knowing full well what she meant. This was, after all, a conversation that occurred almost daily. "You know that. And no-one will."

"They mustn't," Patience replied. "She's still there, you know."

"You don't have to worry about any of this," Anne told her. "Why don't you let me help you back to bed? I'm making some soup for lunch, and I know you like that."

"I don't want people to forget," Patience told her, paying little attention as Anne put the rest of the jewelry away and took her by the hand. "That must never be allowed to happen."

"It certainly won't," Anne said, leading her slowly across the room. "You know you can trust me on that matter."

"But how can you be sure?" Patience asked.

"You'll just have to trust that I can," Anne replied.

As they reached the bed, Anne pulled the sheets aside and saw that one had indeed dropped slightly into the bedpan, which needed emptying. She dragged that sheet out from the rest and threw it onto the floor, so that it could be taken down to the washing room, and then she helped Patience ease back down onto the bed.

"I'll be back up with another sheet for you," she said, before picking up the bedpan and taking a step back. "Don't worry about -"

"Where's Daniel?" Patience replied, her

milky white eyes catching glints of the sun from the window. "Can you ask him to come up and see me when he has time? I want to talk to him about that house, we really must find a permanent solution."

"Grandfather -"

Anne hesitated, but deep down she already knew that this was not the right day to try dragging Patience back to reality. In general, she preferred to let her grandmother live in her own little world, and she knew the old woman's memories seemed to reset every few hours anyway. Patience was always asking for her long-dead husband, but she never thought that he'd been gone for more than a few hours at a time.

"I'll be back up shortly," she said finally, struggling to hold back tears as she forced a smile. "Stay in your bed this time. When I come back, I don't want to find you bumbling around on your own. Is that clear?"

CHAPTER TWO

"BUT *WHERE* DOES IT all come from?"

Standing on the road outside the village pub, opposite the rotten old hanging posts, Molly looked up into the vast white sky and watched as more and more snow drifted down. She blinked every time a flake landed in her eyes, but she couldn't help simply staring at the bright void that carpeted the sky in every direction.

Finally she turned and saw that Charlotte was using a stick to draw crumbling lines in a pile of snow near the wall.

"What are you doing?"

"Nothing," Charlotte replied, furrowing her brow a little. "I can't wait to be an adult, so that I won't be so bored all the time."

"But then you'll have to work," Molly pointed out. "You'll probably have to get married and look after your husband, and he'll expect you to give birth to children."

"I suppose so," Charlotte said with a sigh.

"And all the boys in Cobblefield are ugly," Molly added, "and I don't expect that any of them will get any more handsome as they grow older."

"I suppose not."

"Even if they do," Molly continued, turning and looking at the windows of *The Shoemaker*, "they'll just drink too much like every other man here."

She listened for a moment to the sound of voices coming from inside the pub, and then she turned to Charlotte again.

"Your father's a good example of that," she pointed out. "*My* father says that yours is a horrid drunk who's good for nothing. He says he's never seen a man who's so poor at just about any task he turns his hand to, and he says the only reason Horace isn't destitute and on the streets is because he married into your mother's family. And at least they own the stables, and..."

Her voice trailed off for a moment.

"And a house outside the village," she added.

"I suppose so."

"I've heard strange stories about that house," Molly continued. "Some people say it's haunted."

"I suppose so."

"Is that all you've got to say about anything?" Molly asked, stepping closer. "I've heard that no-one has been near that house in more than a thousand years, because they're all scared of that ghost that lives there." She watched Charlotte's face for a reaction. "Apparently the ghost is really scary and mean, and anyone who looks into its eyes is cursed to eternal damnation."

Charlotte shrugged.

"Do you want to go and see?" Molly added.

Charlotte turned to her.

"Why not?" Molly continued. "There's nothing else to do in this boring village. You said it yourself, you don't want to be bored all the time, so why not take matters into your own hands?" Spotting movement nearby, she turned and saw Peter Finch – a boy she knew from church – walking along the street. "Hey, Peter," she called out, "do you want to do something fun?"

"Like what?" Peter asked, stopping nearby with his hands in his pockets. "Play with sticks in the snow? That doesn't seem like much fun to me."

"I'm not talking about that," Molly replied,

allowing herself a faint smile. "I'm talking about something that's much more fun. Did you know that Charlotte's family own a big scary house outside the village?"

Peter thought for a moment, and then he shook his head.

"Well?" Molly continued with a mischievous glint in her eye. "Why don't we go and see for ourselves?"

***

As more snow fell, the three children made their way to the bottom of the sloping road that led out toward the north-west of the village. They stopped for a moment, all three of them watching the forest, and for a few seconds they seemed to be each privately contemplating the enormity of the trek that lay ahead of them.

"It's not *that* far," Molly said finally.

"How do you know?" Peter asked, before reaching down and picking up a stone from the ground. He examined it, and then he slipped it into a cloth bag he took from his pocket.

"What's that for?" Charlotte asked.

"I keep the ones I like," he told her, a little shyly. "I just like collecting them."

"Do you know how far it is?" Molly said, turning to Charlotte.

Charlotte merely shook her head.

"Why not?" Molly continued. "Doesn't your family own the house?"

"That doesn't mean I know anything about it," Charlotte said, and now she sounded a little more uncomfortable than before. "I promised my mother that I wouldn't go too far from home and -"

"Your mother's always too busy dealing with your drunk father," Molly pointed out, cutting her off. "Everyone knows that's true. Don't they, Peter?"

"I heard that Horace Smudge hasn't been sober for one second in the last ten years," Peter said. "That's what people are telling each other."

"He's not that bad," Charlotte replied, although deep down she knew that he was right.

"We have to follow the road," Molly told them, returning her attention to the forest, "and then find a dirty little track that leads off between the trees. I heard someone talking about it once. After we find that track, we follow it and eventually we'll come to a big wall and a gate, and that's Hadlow House." She paused, before taking a deep breath. "I'm bored of waiting," she added finally. "Only scared little children wait. Are you two coming with me, or not?"

"I'm going to go home," Charlotte told her.

"Are you too scared?"

"No!"

"Then why aren't you coming?" Molly asked, before turning to Peter. "What about you? Are you a scared little girl like Charlotte?"

"No!" he protested, although after a moment he appeared slightly hesitant, as if he'd suddenly realized that he'd agree to something unnerving. "I mean... I just don't see that there's any point in going out there. If there's no-one living in the house, it's just a big boring pile of bricks."

"If that's true, then there's no reason to be scared," Molly said firmly, fixing him with a pointed stare. Clearly trying to read between the lines, she watched him for a moment. "You don't have to come, Peter," she added, "but if you don't, I'll tell everyone that you were too afraid."

"I'm not afraid!"

"Then let's go," she continued, stepping forward and starting to make her way along the road. "You don't want to still be there when it gets dark, do you? I know I don't, so let's hurry up!"

Peter opened his mouth to call after her, but he quickly realized that there was no point. He hesitated, and then with a sigh he set off.

"Come on," he muttered to Charlotte. "Let's just get this over with."

"I don't think it's a good idea," Charlotte replied, but she already knew that the time had come to make a decision. She was deeply regretting her decision to leave the house, and she couldn't help worrying that she was about to get in a lot of trouble, but at the same time she also wanted to impress her friends.

Glancing over her shoulder, she looked at the village for a moment, and then – making a split-second decision – she hurried off after Molly and Peter.

"Wait for me!" she called out, already struggling up the sloping road. "Can you please wait for me? Hey, shouldn't we all do this together?"

Once she caught up to Peter, she slowed to match his pace. Her ankles were already aching and deep down she knew she was making a big mistake, but she told herself that she was sick and tired of being mostly ignored by the other children in the village. People already gossiped enough about her family – about her drunk father and her crazy great-grandmother and about the weird house in the forest – and she wanted to prove that she was more normal. She wanted to show everyone that she was just like them.

"How long's it going to take to get to this house?" Peter asked breathlessly.

"Tired already?" Molly called back to him.

"I just want to know!"

"It'll take as long as it takes," she replied. "Two hours, I think, if we don't make any mistakes and end up lost. I bet you don't want to get lost in this forest, do you?"

"This house had better be worth it," Peter muttered, keeping his voice so low that only Charlotte could hear him. "It'd better be really spooky and really scary and worth the effort. It probably won't be, though. It'll probably just be a big disappointment, like everything else anywhere near this stupid village."

Keeping her thoughts to herself, Charlotte simply focused on keeping up with her two friends. She knew that the house was waiting out there somewhere in the forest, and she just hoped that they could get close and then immediately turn around. Looking over her shoulder, she told herself that hopefully her mother would be far too busy to realize that she was even gone. After all, for as long as she could remember, she'd always been told that no member of her family was ever allowed to go anywhere near Hadlow House ever again.

CHAPTER THREE

"AND I'VE TOLD YOU before," Anne said firmly as she stood at the front door of Cobblefield Stables, "it's not for sale."

"Perhaps I haven't been sufficiently clear," Mr. Wadsworth said, before clearing his throat. "I don't suppose your husband might be home soon, might he? This sort of business is best discussed between men."

"*I'm* the owner of Hadlow House," she reminded him, "and I'm perfectly able to listen to your foolish offers and give you an answer. Which I've already done."

"You won't get a better offer," Mr. Wadsworth continued, clearly struggling to remain polite. "If you think you can hold out -"

"Let me spell this out in a way that you can't fail to comprehend," she said, interrupting him. "Hadlow House is not for sale, and that isn't going to change. There's no need for you to lecture me on the value of the property, or the value of the land, or anything like that. When I took ownership of the house from my grandmother, I explicitly promised her that I would never let it be sold, and there's nothing you can do to make me go against my word."

"The money -"

"The money is inconsequential."

"I still think that I should speak to your husband," he told her. "He might have a more... sophisticated understanding of the transaction that I'm proposing. My client -"

"Your client will have to look elsewhere," she said, cutting him off yet again. "Mr. Wadsworth, this is the third time you have come to my door in as many months, and I have told you the same thing on each occasion. I don't mean to be rude, but if you come again I shall simply refuse to answer when you knock. As for my husband, you might well linger and try to talk to him without me, but I can assure you that he will have no better luck trying to persuade me to change my mind. He has already tried and failed numerous times."

"If -"

"Good day, Mr. Wadsworth," she added, taking a step back and putting a hand on the side of the door. "I am about to close this," she told him. "Please, to avoid any risk that I might seem rude, turn and walk away."

She waited for a moment, before finally shutting the door anyway. Taking a deep breath, she leaned forward and gently rested her forehead against the wood, and at that moment she breathed a sigh of relief as she heard the infernal man walking away across the yard. She had tried being subtle with him, she had tried being direct, and now she had tried being rude. She could only hope that he and his mysterious client would finally get the message.

"Are you sure you haven't made a mistake?" Horace asked.

Turning, she saw him watching her from the kitchen.

"We could use the money for the business," he continued, "and if we're honest, we both know that there's not anything actually dangerous in that house. And if you're worried about old Patience, I really don't think there's any need. It's not like she actually knows what's happening in the world anyway, so she doesn't even have to find out. She's about as sane as a box of squirrels."

"I have work to do," she replied, turning and pushing past him on her way into the kitchen. "As do you, if you're sober enough. Have you seen Charlotte, by the way? She's supposed to be playing in the street."

"Anne, the money would -"

"I'm not talking about it again," she said firmly as she stopped at the sink. She paused, feeling a growing sense of anger starting to simmer in her chest. "And you're wrong about Patience," she added after a moment. "You think she wouldn't know, but she would. Don't ask me how it works, but she'd sense it somehow. I would never, ever dare to even *try* to hide something like that from her, and I would like you to remember that next time before you speak." She paused to look out the window, watching the rear yard for a moment. "She'd know," she whispered. "When it comes to that house, she'd always know if it was in any way disturbed."

***

"She's mad, is what she is," Horace muttered angrily as he sat in *The Shoemaker* and contemplated his pint of beer. "All that money just waiting to be given to us, and all she has to do is sign over the deeds to that house, but will she? Hell, of course she won't. She's just being stubborn!"

"I've known that family for a while," his friend James Leash said, sitting slumped at the next stool. "There's something wrong with them when it comes to Hadlow House. They've got a blind-spot."

"It's not right," Horace replied. "A house like that shouldn't just sit empty, not when a proper family could be enjoying it. I'm not even fussing solely about the money, it'd be nice but I'm not a greedy man." He took another sip of beer. "I'm thinking more about other people, you see. I'm sure there's a lovely family who'd just love to slide in and make that house their own. Why should they be denied? Just because of some local superstitious nonsense?"

"I've heard it's a bit more than that," James pointed out. "I've never been up there myself, but you hear stories about -"

"You hear stories about all sorts of things," Horace replied, cutting him off. "Do I look like an idiot to you? Don't waste my time with those old wives' tales. That house is a potential goldmine and I don't see why I should have to scrimp and save my way through life when there's all that money just dangling there in front of us." He paused. "All because of that Patience woman."

"You mean your wife's grandmother?"

"She's almost a century old," he explained. "Doesn't that strike anyone as being too much of a life? Who needs to live that long, anyway? She's out of her mind, she can barely even aim at the bedpan properly. There's no dignity for her, she ought to..."

His voice trailed off for a moment.

"Ought to *what* ?" James asked cautiously.

"I'm just saying that I'm sure Patience, if she could see herself sensibly, would agree that the time has come for her to shuffle off this mortal coil. She's only holding things back, anyway, and creating a nuisance." He thought about the idea for a moment. "You know, if she was out of the way, I'm certain I'd be able to talk Anne around and get her to do the right thing. It's just that stupid old hag in the bedroom upstairs who's causing all the problems. How fair is that?"

"Doesn't sound very fair to me," James replied.

Horace glanced around, to make sure that nobody was eavesdropping, and then he leaned a little closer to his friend.

"How long do you think the old bird's got left?" he whispered. "A year? Two? She's been clinging on for a while now, so would it really make any difference if she happened to have a little accident right now? She's holding the entire family back, and Anne's just too stubborn to see it. If you think of it that way, you could even argue that Anne's unnecessarily torturing poor Patience by trying to keep her alive long past her prime."

"What exactly are you suggesting?" James asked. "It almost sounds like..."

His voice trailed off for a moment.

"Perhaps you shouldn't tell me any more," he added after a few seconds. "At least that way, I won't be burdened by any kind of guilt."

"You make a good point," Horace told him, although he couldn't hide a faint, sly smile. "Mark my words, though, that old woman's days are numbered." He took another sip of beer, and then he thought for a moment as he felt the first stages of a plan starting to come together. "I'm actually a very nice fellow," he added under his breath. "I hate to see someone suffer like that. Truly, I think the only decent thing would be to help end old Patience's suffering."

James began to talk to two other men who had just entered the bar, but Horace was barely aware of anyone or anything around him. Instead, his mind was racing as he tried to come up with a foolproof plan, and he was starting to think that there was no point delaying matters for even a moment longer. And after a couple more seconds, he realized that he knew exactly how he was going to help hasten Patience toward her demise.

"It's not about the money," he whispered to himself. "It's about doing the right thing."

CHAPTER FOUR

"ARE YOU SURE WE'RE not lost?" Peter asked, sounding increasingly frustrated as he and Charlotte followed Molly through the forest, struggling through the snow. "I don't think we should go any further. I think we should just turn back and go home."

"You're so scared all the time," Molly said, taunting him as she continued to lead the way. "We're not lost, it's just taking a little longer than it should, that's all."

"I don't know why I keep getting myself into situations like this," Peter said, before turning to Charlotte and watching her face as they walked. "What's wrong with you, anyway? I don't think you've said a single word since we left the village."

"I don't think we should be doing this," she

said softly.

"Why not? Because of your family?"

He stopped and picked up another small stone, taking a moment to slip it into his bag.

"Because there's something bad in the house," Charlotte admitted.

"Do you really believe that?" he asked. "I mean, hand on heart, do you truly believe all the stories that people tell about the place?"

"I don't know," she said shyly, although she quickly realized that she should probably be more honest. "I suppose so."

"I think it's just a bit of fun," he told her. "It's a way for people to scare themselves, so you shouldn't take any of it too seriously. You're just unlucky that it's your family that's at the center of it, that's all. Do you think you'll get into a lot of trouble if your mother and father found out that you've been out here?"

"I definitely will," she admitted.

"Then you're the bravest one out of the three of us," he suggested. "I think the -"

"We've found it!" Molly called out, stopping a few paces ahead and pointing past the trees. "Look, over there! That's the gate!"

Charlotte wanted to tell her that she was wrong, but she quickly saw the name Hadlow House in metal lettering over a large gate built into a brick wall. She felt a shudder run through her body as she realized her last hope – that they'd never find the house at all – had been dashed, and she instinctively clenched and then un-clenched her fists as she battled against a strong desire to turn around and run away.

"See?" Molly said triumphantly. "I told you were weren't lost! Come on!"

She raced ahead, hurrying toward the gate as if this was the most exciting moment in her life. Peter hesitated, clearly a little more concerned, before setting off after her, and after a few seconds Charlotte began to follow as well. Every step felt terribly heavy, and she still wanted to stop, but she found herself clinging to a new hope that perhaps the house would turn out not to be scary at all. As she reached the gate and looked through at Hadlow House, however, she saw its darkened facade and felt a shudder run through her bones.

"Look at it," Molly said, placing her hands on the gate's metal bars as she peered through into the overgrown garden. "Just sitting here for all this time, completely empty. Well, empty except for the ghosts."

"There aren't any ghosts," Charlotte said cautiously.

"Then what are you afraid of?" Molly asked.

"Don't you think it's weird?" Peter muttered. "Look at the windows. Imagine if there really *was* a ghost in there. Would he or she be staring back at us right now?"

"Probably," Molly told him, keeping her eyes fixed on the house. "I suppose they've been bored ever since the last person came here. There can't be much to do when you're a ghost." She paused, before turning the handle and pushing the gate open, causing the rusty hinges to let out a loud creaking sound. "Well," she added with a smile, "if the ghosts didn't know that we were here before, I bet they do now. They must have heard the gate just now." She turned to Charlotte and Peter. "So you're coming with me, aren't you?" she added. "Please, tell me you wouldn't let me go over to the house all by myself."

***

A couple of minutes later, having picked their way along the path that was barely visible beneath so much snow, the three children reached the front of the house. They stopped, looking at the ominous front door, and then Molly walked over to one of the windows.

"Be careful!" Charlotte called after her.

"Why?"

Cupping her hands around her eyes, Molly leaned against the glass and tried to look inside.

"I can't see anything at all," she complained. "It's *so* dark in there, there could be somebody standing right on the other side of this glass right now and staring at me, and I don't think I'd be able to see them."

"Let's hope there isn't anyone there," Peter murmured.

"It seems so still," Molly continued, stepping back and looking at the upstairs windows. "Can't you feel that in the air? It's like you can tell that the house isn't moving at all. I know houses don't really move anyway, but this is something else, it's like... I suppose it might be like when someone's breathing and then they stop, and suddenly something that should be moving... isn't." She turned to the others. "Does that make sense?"

"Shouldn't we go now?" Charlotte asked awkwardly.

"Go?" Molly stared at her incredulously for a moment, before taking a step closer. "Are you out of your mind? We went to all the trouble of finding this place, we can't just walk away now."

"I'm going to be in so much trouble when I get home," Charlotte told her.

"Oh, please," Molly said, rolling her eyes, "why does that even matter? You're not scared of your parents, are you? Your father's a drunk, so he won't care, and your mother will be too busy preparing dinner. Trust me, they'll probably both be glad that you're occupied for the afternoon."

"I don't like it here," Charlotte said, looking

at one of the other windows and imagining a figure standing in the darkness. "Something doesn't feel right."

"That's probably the ghost watching you," Molly replied, stepping over to the front door and giving it a try, only to find that it wouldn't budge. "Your family's connected to this house, so it makes sense that the ghost would recognize you." She turned to Charlotte. "It probably sensed you coming long before we even got here."

"That's not true!" Charlotte said firmly.

"How do you know? I think it sounds very true. How old is this ghost supposed to be, anyway? I bet it's been here for a long time, and it's probably been waiting for someone from your family to show up. Your weird great-grandmother lived here once, didn't she? Before she went mad, I mean. So there's a lot of family history for you tied into this place, and only an idiot would deny that. Are you an idiot, Charlotte?"

"No!" she snapped angrily.

"Calm down," Molly chuckled, "there's no need to react like that. I'm not trying to be mean, I just wanted to point something out to you, that's all."

"We shouldn't argue," Peter said, shivering a little as more snow continued to fall. "We came here, like we promised we would, but Charlotte's right. We should turn around now."

"Not before we go inside," Molly replied.

"No," Charlotte said, shaking her head. "That's too much."

"I'm going to look for a back door," Molly said, picking her way through the snow as she struggled to get round to the side of the house. "There has to be one, and then we can explore the inside of the house. If you two are too scared, you can wait out here or you can go home. I don't mind. But I'm going to take a look inside, because I want to see exactly what's waiting in there."

"She doesn't really believe there's a ghost," Peter said as Molly disappeared around the corner, although her footsteps could still be heard crunching through the snow. "If she did, she wouldn't be so desperate to get inside. She's just trying to show off."

"I really don't like being here," Charlotte told him. "It's not just because I was told not to, it's because I feel like there's something really wrong. I can't explain it, but it's almost like there's something hanging in the air, almost like it's trying to warn us to turn around."

"We'll go soon," he told her, before placing a hand on her shoulder. "I promise."

"Can't we go *now*?"

"We should go and find Molly," he replied, pulling his hand away and turning to walk off around to the back of the house. "She'll never shut up if we don't join her. You know what she's like, she always wants to show off and pretend that she's better than everyone else, and she'll be completely insufferable if she goes into this house and we wait outside." He sighed. "You know I'm right, Charlotte," he added. "Come on, let's just follow her for a few more minutes and then we can tell her we're going home."

Left standing alone in front of the house, Charlotte hesitated for a moment. She desperately wanted to leave immediately, but deep down she knew that she had to keep proving herself for a little while longer. Finally, reluctantly, she began to follow the others, walking carefully in their footsteps in an effort to make her passage through the snow a little easier.

CHAPTER FIVE

"MR. WADSWORTH!" HORACE CALLED out, hurrying across the road and catching the older man just as he was about to climb up into his carriage. "Sir, might I speak with you for a moment?"

"That very much depends upon the nature of your business," Mr. Wadsworth replied, turning to him with a skeptical scowl on his face. "Who are you and what do you want?"

"My name is Horace Smudge," he explained, holding out a hand. "I believe you might have visited my wife Anne today at our home."

"Ah, of course," Mr. Wadsworth replied, shaking his hand with a degree of caution. "I must say that your wife is a very obstinate woman. I made her a very good offer, yet again, but she turned me down. I had hoped to speak with the man

of the house, but I was informed that you were out."
He looked Horace up and down for a moment,
while making no effort to hide his disdain. "Do I
detect the aroma of stale beer?"

"You are absolutely right about my wife,"
Horace told him. "She *is* stubborn, but fortunately I
have certain tricks for winning her over."

"That might be the case," Mr. Wadsworth
told him, "but I have visited her on three occasions
now, and I am afraid that she has consistently turned
me down. I must return to my client and inform him
that he'll have to look elsewhere for a property in
this part of Kent."

"Let us not be too hasty," Horace replied
with a big, broad smile. "You seem like an
intelligent man who knows the way the world
works. I am sure, too, that you know women can be
difficult to handle, but I know how to bring Anne
around to my way of thinking. Please, I beg you not
to give up on the purchase of Hadlow House. What
would you say if I told you that, if you were to
come back in one week's time, you would receive a
much more grateful welcome?"

"Are you proposing to force your wife to
sell that house?"

"Force is a strong word," Horace told him.
"I aim merely to... encourage her to see things from
a different point of view. And I am quite sure that
by the time I am finished, I shall be able to grease

the wheels of any deal."

"I would require a little more certainty than that."

"Then let me be plainer," Horace continued. "I guarantee, Mr. Wadsworth, that if you return to Cobblefield in one week's time I shall have my wife ready to sell Hadlow House. For a fair price, of course. And then everyone will be happy."

"You are sure that you can do this?"

"You have my word on the matter, Sir," Horace told him. "There is shortly to be a change of circumstances in our household, one that will allow me to assert my authority with a little more determination."

***

"Anne?" Horace called out, standing in the front door at Cobblefield Stables and listening to the silence of the house. "My dear, are you at home?"

He waited, but he knew that in all likelihood Anne was out fetching various items from the nearby shops. Her routine was fairly easy to predict, and he supposed that she would be gone for at least one hour, since she always liked to stop and exchange gossip with anyone she met in the street. He hesitated for a few more seconds, just to be sure that his wife wasn't about to emerge from one of the back rooms, and then he shut the door and made his way over to the foot of the stairs.

Again he stopped and listened, and again he heard nothing. He knew, however, that the house was not empty, for Patience had not left the place in more than two decades. She was up there somewhere, perhaps sleeping or perhaps simply pacing around in her room, but he had no doubt whatsoever that she was up to something, and after a few seconds he began to make his way up the staircase while putting the finishing touches to his great plan.

"Poor old Patience," he whispered under his breath, unable to hide a sense of anticipation. "What a wretched life to have to live, suffering so much pain day in and day out. Someone ought to put her out of all this misery."

Reaching the landing, he looked at the door to Patience's room. Part of him wanted to wait, and to perhaps make sure this his plan was perfect, but at the same time he supposed that there was no point delaying things. Besides, he'd already persuaded Mr. Wadsworth to return just one week later, and he knew that he'd need time after Patience's death to talk Anne around, so as he stepped toward the door and turned the handle he told himself to act quickly and decisively.

As soon as he looked into the room, he saw that Patience was in her bed.

"There you are!" he said, trying to sound

jolly and happy as he walked over and pulled the sheets off. "How are you doing today, Patience? Would you like to get up and come for a little walk?"

Looking up at him, Patience opened her mouth as if she was about to say something, but for a few seconds she seemed startled.

"That's right," Horace continued, reaching down and grabbing her hands, then starting to pull her up. "You can't sit around in your room all day like this, that's no way to live your life. Don't you want to move around a little?"

"What do you want from me?" Patience murmured as he hauled her onto her feet and began to lead her toward the door. "Where's Anne?"

"Oh, don't you worry about Anne," he replied, still trying to sound kind and friendly. "Anne's busy doing all the things a wife's supposed to do. You raised her very well, didn't you? She's a real credit to you, Patience. I hope you know that long after you're gone, we're all going to think back very fondly to our time spent with you."

"Where are you taking me?" she asked as they stepped out onto the landing and began to make their way toward the top of the stairs. "I don't know that I feel up to this."

"You'll be fine," he told her. "You're tougher than you look, aren't you? Everyone always treats you as if you're some delicate thing, but I reckon there's more fight to you, Patience. Just because you're an old lady, that doesn't mean you haven't got some fight in you."

"I'm so tired," she murmured. "Where's Daniel?"

"Your late husband?" He chuckled. "Well, you might see him rather soon."

"I don't want to go anywhere," she said, stopping and trying to turn back to go to her room. "I want to rest until Anne comes home."

"You don't really want to do that," he replied, pulling her back toward the top of the stairs and then stepping behind her. "Do you know what you could do with, Patience? More confidence. And it's funny that you mentioned old Daniel there, because from what Anne tells me you and him were properly in love. What's that like? I must confess, sometimes I wonder whether love's a real thing at all."

Again Patience tried to pull away, but Horace was able to maneuver her properly into place at the top of the staircase, and then he took a moment to push her hands down as she tried to support herself against the railing.

"Thank you for everything you've done for this family, Patience," he said through gritted teeth, holding her arms down at her sides with more force now, and no longer trying too hard to hide his intentions. "As I told you, you'll always be remembered with such fondness, and I'll make sure that you're buried close to your mother and father in the graveyard at St. Leonard's. I just hope you realize that today you're doing one final thing that'll make sure your family is always taken care of."

"Wait," she replied, "I want -"

Before she could finish, Horace shoved her hard in the back, sending her toppling over. Letting out a brief cry, Patience tumbled down the stairs, slamming against several of the steps with force until she landed at the bottom in a crumpled, motionless heap. Horace stood at the top, watching her with a calm expression on his face, but after a few more seconds he allowed himself the faintest of smiles as he saw that she was still not moving at all.

"I'm sorry, Patience," he said firmly, "but that had to be done. And now we can move on with our lives, and we don't have to worry about any more silliness regarding that stupid Hadlow House."

CHAPTER SIX

"WHY'S IT LOCKED?" MOLLY muttered, trying the back door yet again before stepping away and looking at the windows with a sigh. "Why bother when no-one wants to come out here anyway?"

"Can we go now?" Charlotte asked, standing a little further away. "Please?"

"I could break a window," Molly said, picking up a small stone from the ground and taking some more steps back. "No-one'll know it was me."

She took a moment to prepare her aim.

"I really don't think you should do this," Peter told her.

"Shut up," she murmured, staring at the kitchen window for a moment as she prepared to strike. She swallowed hard, trying to summon the necessary courage, and then at the last second she sighed heavily and let the stone fall to the ground. "Fine," she said, turning to the others, "you win. I suppose I shouldn't cause any actual damage. One of you would only rat me out eventually."

"We wouldn't!" Charlotte protested.

"Nice try, but I know differently," Molly told her. "You wouldn't be able to live with the guilt, would you? You'd feel compelled to tell someone eventually."

"I wouldn't," Charlotte replied, although deep down she knew that Molly probably had a point.

They stood in silence for a moment, each contemplating the gloomy rear of the house. Having been abandoned for a quarter of a century, Hadlow House appeared rundown and terribly neglected, with twenty-five years' of bad weather having left the windows pocked and dirty, while the wood around the frames had begun to rot a little. Snow was packed against the house on all sides, and in some areas the walls even showed signs of premature damp, while the falling snow hinted at even colder conditions on the other side of the dark, slightly swollen back door.

"Maybe we shouldn't have come out here after all," Molly whispered, as if finally even *she* had been struck by some dark hidden aspect of the house's appearance. "Come on, we should get home while it's still light."

She turned and began to trudge back around the house, stepping carefully into the pits made earlier by her own feet in the snow, and Charlotte and Peter quickly followed. The sound of their footsteps crunching into the snow rang out in the open clearing, emphasizing the stillness all around, and as they reached the front of the house Charlotte had begun to notice that she could hear no other signs of life. She glanced at the trees and wondered whether there were even any birds in the area. All that moved, as far as she could see, was the slowly falling snow.

Bumping against Peter from behind, she turned to him and saw that he'd stopped to look at the front of the house. Molly had done the same, and Charlotte hesitated for a moment before furrowing her brow.

"Are we going?" she asked cautiously.

"Wasn't that..."

Molly's voice drifted off for a moment.

"Wasn't that closed before?" she stammered.

Turning, Charlotte immediately felt a shiver run through her chest as she saw that Hadlow House's front door – which had been so resolutely shut earlier, seemingly locked – was now standing wide open, revealing the darkness of the hallway inside.

"That was closed before," Molly continued. "I tried to lots of times. It was locked."

"You must have been wrong," Peter told her.

"It wouldn't open!" she insisted, keeping her eyes fixed on the doorway. "I'm telling you, it was locked!"

"It can't have been," Peter said. "You're just -"

"It was locked!" she said angrily, before hesitating and then starting to push through the snow again, making her way toward the steps in front of the door. "It must have swung open by itself somehow. A gust of wind might have done it."

"Must have been a strong gust of wind," Peter pointed out, before setting off after her.

"There isn't any wind," Charlotte said. She looked around for a moment, waiting for even the slightest hint of wind to prove her wrong, and then she turned to see that Molly and Peter were both peering in through the front door. "Aren't we going home?" she called out to them, even though she already sensed that she'd lost the argument again. "Molly? Peter? Didn't we just say we were all going to go home before it gets dark? Didn't you say that was a good idea?"

She waited, but her frustration was growing. A moment later Molly stepped fully into the doorway, framed against the darkness within.

"I can see the stairs!" she called out.

"I think I can too," Peter said, stepping up behind her. "It's really spooky in there."

"We said we were going home now," Charlotte reminded them, as she struggled to keep tears from her eyes. "You promised!"

She waited, but after a moment Molly stepped forward and disappeared into the house, followed almost immediately by Peter.

"Don't do that!" Charlotte shouted, before looking around again as she realized that she'd been left all alone. She desperately wanted to turn and walk away, but she was far too scared to go through the forest alone so after a moment she hurried toward the front of the house and looked through the open front door.

At that moment, she saw Molly walked toward the bottom of the staircase, and a fraction of a second later she heard a low creaking sound coming from the floor.

"This board is really loose," Molly said, testing the same spot a couple more times and producing the same sound. "It sounds so loud when there are no other sounds."

"You've been inside now," Charlotte pointed out. "That's what you came to do, and you've done it, so -"

"Listen to it," Molly continued, pushing the same loose floorboard over and over. "It really wobbles!"

"Stop that," Charlotte said, worried that somehow the creaking board was going to ring out throughout the entire house and wake someone up. "You shouldn't do it!"

"Why not?" Molly asked, turning to her with a smile while still pushing on the board.

"Because it's loud!"

"Why does that matter?"

"You might upset someone!"

"Who?" Molly asked, taking extra care to push the board harder than ever. "Who are you worried I might upset, Charlotte?"

"Please just stop!" Charlotte sobbed, as tears began to run down her face. "Molly, please!"

"You're so funny," Molly said, before pulling her foot away from the board, allowing the house to return to its former silence. "I didn't mean to make you cry," she added, although she was still clearly amused by the situation. "I didn't know you were that much of a little baby."

"I'm not a little baby," Charlotte replied, wiping tears from her cheeks. "I just don't think you should have done that. That's all."

"What's in here?" Peter asked, stepping through one of the other doorways and entering a room to the right. "It's really hard to see."

"Can we *please* go now?" Charlotte asked.

"Wait outside if you're too scared," Molly told her, before following Peter. "That's a lot of boxes," she could be heard saying from inside the room. "What do you think's in them all?"

Charlotte waited for a moment, desperately not wanting to actually enter the house. She looked across the hallway and saw no sign of anyone, then she looked up the stairs and saw nothing at all in the darkness. A moment later, hearing the faintest sound of a snapping twig, she turned and looked back out across the snow-covered garden; she waited for a few seconds, and now her heart was racing. She knew she didn't want to go into the house, of course, but she was also far too scared to be alone, so finally she stepped across the threshold and made her way to the door on the right, where she stopped as soon as she saw – in the gloom – Molly and Peter examining a pile of boxes in the corner of what appeared to be some kind of study.

"I wonder who left these here," Peter said, trying to pull the top off from one of the boxes, only to find that it was held on far too tightly. "They look very old."

"Everything here's very old," Molly observed, looking around the room. "And dirty. And untidy. It looks like no-one tidied up before they left. Wasn't there some kind of fight here? I'm sure someone mentioned a gun fight with an American man who wanted to blow up the king. Something like that, anyway."

"It doesn't matter what happened here in the past," Charlotte told them, almost begging her friends now to leave. "It's all done and over. Can't we please leave, though? I'm scared of not getting home while it's still light."

"Listen to the stupid little girl," Molly replied, turning to her with a smile. "We're going to have a look around now we're here, Charlotte. There's obviously nothing here, not even a ghost. Honestly, what's the worst that could possibly happen?"

CHAPTER SEVEN

TOO SCARED TO EVEN breathe, Anne pulled back into the darkness of the small cupboard into which she'd just crawled. Having scurried around trying to find somewhere to hide, and having occasionally spotted a glimpse of the terrifying woman, she had now taken refuge in one of the low cupboards in the kitchen's far corner. There was barely enough space for her to squeeze into, but she'd just about managed to pull the door shut and now she was praying that she hadn't been spotted.

A moment later she heard the slow, low creaking sound of a nearby door being pushed open.

"Please," Anne said silently, hoping that somehow she might be heard by some higher power, "get me out of here."

Now, twenty-five years after that terrifying day when she'd been trapped in Hadlow House, Anne Smudge sat on a pew at the back of St. Leonard's Church with her hands clasped together in prayer. She'd never truly been able to put those awful events out of her mind for long, but for the most part she'd been able to battle against them and push them to the very back of her mind; now, however, she found that for some reason they were threatening to burst back into her thoughts with renewed strength, and she had stepped into the church in the hope of finding some new inner strength.

Yet the memories persisted...

"My child," she heard a cold, dead voice saying finally, drifting through to her from so many years earlier, "why do you run from me like this? Don't you know that it's futile?"

Reaching up, Anne clamped a trembling hand over her own mouth, trying to make sure that she couldn't let out another inadvertent scream.

Startled, Anne realized now that she had done the same thing; entirely involuntarily, she had clamped a hand over her own mouth, twenty-five years after she had made the same move while hiding in that cupboard. This time, she even felt fresh tears filling her eyes, and after a moment she let out a brief, abrupt sob as she leaned forward in the pew. For a few seconds, her entire body shook as she found the memories of that shocking day starting to overtake her senses.

"My dear?"

Turning, she looked up and saw a man standing next to her in the church, although she had to blink a couple of times before she recognized him as Father Walker, the priest who had taken over from Father Brown some years earlier.

"I was working in one of the rooms at the back," Father Walker told her, "and I thought I heard that somebody was out here. Do you mind if I join you, or would you rather be alone?"

"Father, please," she replied, "I would welcome your kind advice."

Smiling gently, Father Walker took a seat on the end of the pew and looked toward the altar. For a moment, they both sat in silent contemplation, although Anne was still sniffing back tears as she struggled to contain her fears.

"This is as very calm place, is it not?" Father Walker observed finally. "I find that the mere act of sitting here can often make all the worries of the world seem less... insistent, somehow." He paused, before turning to her. "My child, what troubles you?"

"It's..."

Her voice trailed off.

"I know a little of your family's history," he told her cautiously. "Father Brown used to tell me of the local community. I have never broached the subject with you directly before, because I was not sure whether it was something you wanted to talk about."

"I don't know why it's affecting me today," she replied, sounding a little out of breath. "I can usually forget about it, more or less, but in the past hour or so it has all returned unbidden to the very front of my thoughts. Why is that, Father?"

"Has something else perhaps unsettled you?"

"I can think of nothing."

"You are a good, churchgoing woman, Anne Smudge," he told her. "I know there are certain... difficulties... concerning your husband, but you navigate such challenges in a manner that I am sure pleases the Lord. It is not my place to interfere in your ways, but I might suggest that any misgivings you currently feel might be connected to doubts or concerns you might have about certain people who are in your life."

"My grandmother always feared that something from Hadlow House could reach out to us here in the village," she told him, worried that she might yet be broaching an irreligious and sinful subject. "I mostly dismissed such concerns, but now I find myself worrying..."

"Then pray," he replied after a moment. "The Lord will keep you safe, Anne Smudge, so long as you pray for guidance. And I can assure you, it is my deeply held belief that you will be protected and guided for as long as you keep the Lord's words in your thoughts."

"But is it wrong of me to consider the possibility?" she asked, her voice filled with fear now. "The possibility that this evil exists in Hadlow House, and that it could reach out to us, and that it could harm us in some way, is... is that counter to everything the Lord teaches us?"

"There are matters we cannot truly understand," he told her, with a hint of darkness in his expression. "We must simply trust in the Lord. He will keep us safe."

***

Standing opposite *The Shoemaker*, barely noticing the snow that continued to fall all around her, Anne stared up at the hanging posts. These posts had been in the village since long before she was born, although she could only remember having seen them used once.

"Good afternoon," Eleanor Finch said, making her way past. "Lost in contemplation, are you?"

Anne turned to her, and for a moment she wasn't quite sure what to say, not even to a woman she considered to be a good friend.

"I know the feeling," Eleanor said, stopping for a moment. "I heard your Horace was out again last night, raising his voice and singing all the way home. I don't know how you manage to put up with him." She glanced around. "I don't suppose you've seen my young Peter, have you? I sent him out to do a few things, but as usual he seems to have become distracted and gone off with some other boys."

"I haven't seen him," Anne replied, "or my Charlotte, for that matter. No doubt they're getting up to some mischief together."

"I shall have his father punish him when he gets home," Eleanor muttered, although she seemed a little amused as she turned and continued on her way. "These children are so very difficult to control, are they not? I'm sure I was much better behaved when I was their age."

"Me too," Anne murmured, before turning to look up at the hanging posts again. "I fear -"

Suddenly she saw a rotten body hanging from one of the posts. A man's dead face was staring down at her; his features had been picked clean by the crows, and his eyes bulged from their sockets as the rope pulled tighter and tighter around his neck. Realizing that this was the same dead man she had seen hanging from the post when she was a child, an American who had been caught by some of the local men, Anne nevertheless took a step back even as she tried to convince herself that she was imagining things. Finally, unable to look any longer, she turned away as the stench of rotten flesh filled her nostrils. For a few seconds this stench remained, before passing as quickly as it had arrived.

Slowly, Anne turned and looked back up at the hanging posts and saw to her relief that the dead man was gone. She immediately made the sign of the cross against her chest, relieved that this horror – wherever it might have come from – had at least faded away, and then she turned again to make her way home.

"Help me!" the dead man gasped, lunging at her and pushing her back. "My soul! Help me!"

She opened her mouth to scream, but in that moment Anne saw that the man was already gone. She looked around but there was no sign of him, and then she hurried on, pushing through the snow as she determined to get home and wait for her mind to settle.

"There are matters we cannot truly understand," she heard Father Walker's voice saying, echoing in her thoughts from just a short while earlier as she reached the yard and made for the front door. "We must simply trust in the Lord. He will keep us safe."

"Indeed," she stammered, pushing the door open, "and -"

Stopping suddenly, she let another horrified gasp as she saw Horace kneeling on the floor at the bottom of the stairs, leaning over Patience's crumpled body.

"My darling!" Horace stammered. "I can explain!"

CHAPTER EIGHT

YET ANOTHER LOOSE BOARD on the stairs creaked as Charlotte reached the top, where she stopped to see that Molly and Peter were already exploring two of the bedrooms. She looked around, but the top floor of Hadlow House seemed – if anything – even more unwelcoming than the rest.

"There are holes in this door," Molly pointed out, swinging one of the bedroom doors closed a little so that the others can see. "Guns were fired in here once."

"Wait," Peter replied, turning to Charlotte, "wasn't your great-grandfather one of the men killed when..."

His voice trailed off as he realized the full horror of what he'd been about to say.

"I think so," Charlotte said awkwardly,

looking around and wondering where exactly Daniel Purkiss had fallen after he'd been shot. Or had he been shot downstairs? She'd heard the story, but now the details escaped her, yet she shuddered as she thought of such a terrible thing having happened at all.

"I don't think he was the only one who died that night," Molly said, swinging the door again, causing the hinges to creak loudly. "I heard there was a big battle and twenty or thirty people were killed."

"It wasn't that many," Peter replied.

"Wasn't it? How do you know? Were you there?"

"Can you stop doing that?" Charlotte asked, hating the sound of the door's creaking hinges.

"Why?" Molly said with a smile.

"You might upset someone."

"Who?"

"I don't know."

"Is there anyone else here?" Molly called out, raising her voice. "Is there anyone else here in Hadlow House who doesn't like us making some noise? If there's anyone else here, let us know by banging something loudly to make us stop!"

She waited, still causing the hinges to creak, and then she smiled once more at Charlotte.

"See?" she continued. "You're just getting scared over nothing."

"Then stop it," Charlotte said darkly.

"Fine," Molly muttered, before flinging the door open until it thudded hard against the wall, then stepping out of the bedroom and back onto the landing. "This house is boring, anyway. I don't know whether I really thought there might be a ghost here, but now it's obvious that it's just a big old empty house and everyone's scared of it for no reason. What's wrong, Charlotte? You look like you might be about to soil yourself."

"You don't know what you're talking about," Charlotte replied.

"Are you sure about that?" Molly paused, before stepping past Peter and heading toward her. "I've heard plenty of things about this house from my parents," she added. "I've overheard them talking about it. And one of the things they said was that everyone in your family knows they have to stay away, because there's something here that hates your family more than it hates anyone or anything else. Did you hear that part of the story?" Stopping directly in front of Charlotte, she looked straight into her eyes before using one finger to prod her in the chest. "Peter and I are fine here, it's *you* who needs to worry, because its your family that the ghost of Hadlow House hates so much."

"That's not true," Charlotte said, although her voice betrayed the doubts that filled her mind.

"Isn't it?" Molly paused, before taking a step

back. "Maybe it is, or maybe it isn't, but either way I think you should maybe not have come today. It's almost like you want to get into trouble, and I'm not talking about the trouble you get into when your parents are angry at you. I'm talking about more serious trouble."

"We should go now," Peter told them both.

"That's fine by me," Molly continued. "We've proved that Charlotte's an idiot, so now -"

Suddenly they all heard a loud banging sound coming from somewhere downstairs. Gasping, they all turned and backed against the wall, looking at the top of the stairs as silence returned to the house, but for a few more seconds nobody dared to say a word.

"What was that?" Molly whispered.

Charlotte clenched her teeth.

"I don't know," Peter said, before stepping forward and looking down at the hallway. He stared for a moment before turning to the others. "The front door."

"What?"

"It's shut now," he continued. "I think that was the noise, it was the front door slamming shut."

Molly swallowed hard, before making her way over to join him. Looking down at the door, she saw that he was right.

"Then it was just the wind," she said, with a trace of uncertainty in her voice. "I can't believe you two idiots were scared by that. It was just the wind blowing the door shut, the same way it blew it open earlier. If you think about it, it makes total sense. I can't believe you even let yourselves get scared by something so simple."

She hesitated, and then she stepped forward and began to make her way down the stairs, clearly trying to prove to them that she was brave.

"See?" she continued. "There's really nothing to be scared about."

Reaching the front door, she grabbed the handle, only to find that it seemed once again to be locked. She tried a couple more times, but the door remained firmly shut and finally – as first Peter and then Charlotte followed her down – she took a step back.

"It's stuck again," she complained.

"Let me try."

Peter walked past her and tried the door himself, only to find that she was right.

"What's wrong with this place?" Molly muttered. "First we can't get in, then we can't get out, it's almost as if..."

Her voice trailed off, and she looked a little uncomfortable as she shoved Peter out of the way and tried the door again. This time she was much more forceful, jiggling the handle so hard that the metal and wood rattled together, while muttering under her breath as she tried – increasingly poorly –

to hide the fact that she was starting to panic. Finally she took hold of the handle with both hands, almost shaking it as the door defiantly refused to budge.

"Molly," Peter said, "I think -"

Suddenly the handle came loose, and Molly stumbled back before tripping and landing hard against the bottom of the staircase. Letting out a cry of pain, she dropped the broken handle and rolled onto her side, while touching the small of her back.

"Are you okay?" Charlotte asked, stepping over to her and kneeling down. "What -"

"It hurts!" Molly shouted, shoving her away as tears filled her eyes and began to roll down her cheeks. "I hate you both so much! I just want to go home!"

"Pulling the door handle off didn't help," Peter said, stepping over to the door and examining what was left of the handle. He tried to get the door to move, and then he turned and looked across the hallway. He could see an open door on the other side of the space, opening out into what appeared to be a large kitchen. "There might be a key in the back door."

"How badly does it hurt?" Charlotte asked, reaching over to Molly again. "Can I -"

"Leave me alone!" Molly snapped, hitting her hard in the chin with the base of her hand, sending her falling back. "Don't touch me!"

"I was only trying to help," Charlotte told her.

"Don't get angry," Peter told Molly, stepping over to her. "What -"

"Go away!" Kicking out at him, Molly managed to hit his knee with the heel of her foot, forcing him back. "You're both being horrible to me and I want to go home! I don't want to be in this stupid house anymore! We never should have come here!"

"I'm going to look at the back door," Peter said, heading around past Charlotte. "You can do what you want."

"It really hurts!" Molly sobbed, with tears pouring down her face now as her bottom lip began to tremble. Sitting up, she managed to haul herself onto one of the steps while still rubbing the base of her back. "If you two weren't so stupid, that door would never have shut. Why didn't you put something in the way to stop it?"

"Why didn't *you*?" Charlotte asked meekly.

"Shut up!" Molly hissed, before slamming her fist into the bottom the railing. "Everyone just leave me alone until you've found a way for us to get out of here!"

"You don't have to be so angry," Charlotte told her.

"Go away!" Molly yelled, before taking off one of her own shoes and throwing it hard at

Charlotte, who only just managed to duck out of the way in time. "I'm tired of both of you! You're so stupid!"

"I'm going to go and help Peter," Charlotte said as she turned and began to walk through to the kitchen. "It's not our fault we're all stuck in here, Molly. You're the one who -"

"Shut up! Shut up! Shut up!" Molly screamed at the top of her lungs, slamming her fists into the step as she was left alone. Tears were still rolling down her cheeks, and after a moment she leaned forward and put her hands over her face. "I just want to go home!" she cried. "Why are we stuck here in this stupid, crumbling old house?"

CHAPTER NINE

"GRANDMOTHER?" ANNE GASPED, DROPPING to her knees and reaching down to check for a pulse. "Grandmother, say something!"

"It's too late," Horace told her.

"Grandmother," Anne continued as tears began to run down her cheeks, "talk to me! Say -"

"You're becoming hysterical!" Horace snapped.

"Grandmother, if -"

"No!" Horace shouted, slapping her hard on the side of the face and shoving her back, before stepping around behind her and grabbing her by the shoulders. As she struggled, he pulled her back across the hallway and then dropped to his knees behind her and held her firmly. "It's too late!" he snapped angrily. "She's dead!"

"No!" Anne sobbed.

"She fell down the stairs," he said, before placing an arm across his wife's chest so that she couldn't possibly crawl back over to the body. "I'm sorry, but accidents happens and you know she was unsteady on her feet!"

"Grandmother!" Anne whimpered, before slumping against him and bursting into a series of deep, convulsive sobs. "What was she doing out of bed?"

"I don't know," Horace replied, trying to sound completely innocent as he looked back over at Patience's crumpled figure. "I don't suppose we'll ever be able to find out, but it doesn't really matter. What matters is that she fell and I think she broke her neck, and now we just need to arrange for her burial." He paused for a moment. "Then we should think about that house. I know she said it should be left alone, my darling, but now that she's gone I think we should give serious consideration to selling it. I'm certain we can still get a good price."

"I should have been here," Anne cried, staring in shock at Patience's body. "Why wasn't I here?"

"This was bound to happen eventually," Horace told her. "Why, I just came in from the yard and there she was, all laid out like that. Listen, I think Mr. Wadsworth will be back next week, and by then we need to have made the right decision.

All we have to do is sell Hadlow House, and then it's somebody else's problem. Meanwhile, we can forget about all this backbreaking work and try to live more comfortably!"

"She was relying on me to keep her safe," Anne said, her voice trembling with emotion.

"None of this means we should simply take the first offer, though," Horace said, still holding her tight. "If that Mr. Wadsworth realizes that we're keen to sell all of a sudden, he might try to swindle us. Ideally, we want to get a few different people bidding against each other. Don't worry, though, you can leave all of that in my hands. I'll work out exactly how to handle things." He paused again. "I don't think we really need to go to the expense of a church burial for her, though," he added. "She wouldn't want that."

"She used to be a chimney girl," Anne said, sniffing back more tears. "When she was young and living in London, I mean. She used to tell me about those days, about her life long before she ever came to Cobblefield. I could never imagine her doing that, but she told me all about how she used to wriggle her way up and down chimneys to clean them. She lived such a long life."

"Ninety-nine's more than enough for anyone," Horace muttered, before letting go of his wife and standing up, then brushing his hands clean. "There's nothing more for it now, than for us to move on. That's what she would've wanted. I'll see about getting a grave dug in one of the fields."

"I can't believe she's gone," Anne said, shaking her head as she stared at the body on the floor. "I was supposed to look after her, the way she looked after me when I was a little girl. I should never have let her out of my sight."

"Well, you did," Horace replied, "and now look what's happened. Still, I don't blame you too much. Obviously it was your fault, there's no denying that, but we don't need to make big deal about that. I'm sure you'll learn." He paused for a moment, wondering exactly how to drive his point home further. "You'll just have to accept that she's gone now," he continued, "and that you can't undo anything that happened here. If -"

"She moved!"

"What are you -"

"She moved!" Anne shouted, scrambling across the room and then dropping down next to Patience and nudging her shoulder. "Horace, go and fetch Doctor Cartwright!"

"You're deluded," he replied. "Woman, you're letting your guilt overwhelm you, she's not -"

Before he could get another word out, Patience did indeed twitch slightly, and a fraction of a second later she let out a low, pained groan.

"Fetch Doctor Cartwright!" Anne yelled. "Horace, why are you standing there looking so shocked? Go and get help!"

***

"Stupid old woman," Horace muttered a few minutes later, as he paced back and forth just around the corner from the yard, where he was sure Anne wouldn't be able to see him. "Why couldn't you just die?"

Stopping, he leaned back against the wall and tried to get his thoughts straight. He'd been so utterly sure that Patience was dead, he'd even begun to think about the cheapest and easiest way to dispose of her body, yet now apparently the fall down the stairs hadn't quite been sufficient to finish her off. His mind was racing as he thought of all that wonderful money from the sale of Hadlow House, and he felt a desperate sinking feeling as he realized that Patience's survival put all of that prosperity in jeopardy. He wanted to throttle the old bitch, and a moment later he realized that – actually – throttling her might not be the worst idea.

Indeed, as he imagined wrapping his hands around her throat and squeezing tight, he supposed that he might even enjoy the process.

"Help me!" she imagined her gasping. "Somebody..."

"There's nobody here who can help you now," he thought of himself snarling, crushing her neck with such force that the bones began to break. "This time you're going away, Patience, and there'll be no coming back!"

Or would there? He'd been so sure that she was dead after her tumble down the stairs, and now he worried about the same thing happening again. He could squeeze her neck as tight as he wanted, but what if she once again cheated death? He knew that he needed to be far more certain this time, and after a moment he thought of the various tools and knives in the workshop. Some of those knives, he knew thanks to the cuts on his hands, were plenty sharp, and he supposed that he could quite easily cut the old woman's throat and then wrap a scarf or something around the wound to keep it from view. Then all he had to do was get rid of the body as quickly as possible, before anyone might get a chance to poke around too closely. As a slow smile spread across his face, he realized that this was the plan he should have gone with all along.

"A knife," he said under his breath. "Yes, that's what I need to do. I shall slit her throat from ear to ear."

He thought of that prospect for a moment, before turning to head back to the yard, only to almost slam straight into a man who was walking around the other corner.

"Doctor Cartwright!" he gasped.

"Mr. Smudge," Cartwright replied, clearly

unimpressed by the merest sight of him. "Are you engaged in your usual level of hard work?"

"Oh, you know me," Horace said, realizing that the doctor's route was about to take him directly past the yard, in which case he might be spotted by Anne at one of the windows. "And you, Sir? Out for a walk?"

"I have a few patients to call upon," Cartwright explained, before stepping past him. "I think -"

"I wouldn't go that way, Sir," Horace said, grabbing him by the arm and leading him around the other corner. "There's been a terrible spill outside the butchery, and you wouldn't want your nice shoes getting blood on them, would you? Why don't you take the next lane and go around that way?"

"I suppose so," Cartwright muttered, heading off in that direction. "Thank you, Mr. Smudge. Your warning is most appreciated."

"No trouble at all, Sir," Horace replied, breathing a sigh of relief as he realized that he'd almost accidentally let the doctor go near Patience. "Have a nice day, now. I'm sure you will."

He watched as Doctor Cartwright disappeared from view, before turning and hurrying back toward the yard. Already his mind was filling with details of his plan, and he told himself that this time Patience would be dead within the hour.

CHAPTER TEN

"IT'S BIG IN HERE," Charlotte said as she stepped into the large, gloomy kitchen that ran along the rear side of Hadlow House. "I've never seen such a huge kitchen."

"This back door's stuck too," Peter muttered, trying the handle one more time before turning and looking around. "There's no sign of a key, either. The windows seem to be jammed as well, I don't know why but..."

He paused for a few seconds.

"There's nothing for it," he added. "We're going to have to try to break our way out."

"What do you mean?" Charlotte asked.

"I mean we need to break a window."

"But..."

She turned and looked at the various

windows, all of which were covered in dirt and grime from many decades of neglect.

"They're not big enough," she pointed out. "We'd have to break the wood between some of the bits of glass, and pull it all out to make a larger space."

"Then that's what we'll do."

"I don't think we should."

"Then what's the alternative?" he asked, sounding more than a little frustrated. "I think the sun's already starting to go down a little, soon it'll be dark. We have to get out of here before then."

"But if we break the window, then someone will surely know that we were here." She thought for a moment, trying to think of a better solution. "What if we wait for the wind?" she asked finally.

"The wind?"

"It blew the door open once, and then it blew it closed again. Why don't we wait for it to blow it open again?"

"That could take ages."

"It doesn't have to," she said, sounding somewhat desperate now. "It might just happen in a minute or two if we're patient, and then we'll be able to leave and no-one will ever have to know that we were here at all. I really think we should give that a try."

"Or we might be stuck here forever."

"At least we wouldn't have to break

anything," she pointed out, before pausing again. "I just don't want to get into any trouble, that's all," she continued as she felt fresh tears welling in her eyes. "My parents have told me so many times not to come out here, and I know they were right. They're going to be so angry and disappointed when they realize that I didn't listen."

"If they're anything like *my* parents," he replied, "then they'll be angrier still if I'm back after dark. Why don't we ask Molly what she thinks?"

"I suppose we should," Charlotte said, turning and heading back to the doorway that led into the hall. "Molly?" she called out, looking toward the bottom of the stairs. "Do you think we should break the windows to get out?"

She waited, but – hearing no answer – she quickly made her way across the hall until she reached the bottom of the staircase, at which point she realized that there was no sign of Molly at all. She looked around, but she couldn't see her in any of the rooms, either.

"What's wrong?" Peter called out, making his way out to join her. "Where's Molly?"

"I don't know," Charlotte said, staring down at the empty bottom steps of the staircase. "She was just here a minute ago."

***

"Molly!" Charlotte called out as she stood on the landing, looking around at the various open doors leading into different bedrooms. "Where are you? It's going to get dark soon and we really have to get going."

She waited, but she heard nothing in response.

"Molly?" Peter said downstairs, walking from room to room. "Is this some kind of joke? Are you trying to scare us? If you are, it's not going to work!"

"Molly, just come out," Charlotte muttered, heading to one of the bedrooms and looking through at an old wooden bed. She tried to work out whether there was anywhere Molly might be hiding, and then she walked over to another doorway and looked into the next room. "Molly, I'm tired," she continued. "This isn't very much fun. Coming out here was all your idea, so why are you ruining it now?"

Again she waited, before turning to try another room. At the last second, however, she heard a faint rustling sound coming from behind the door. Stepping into the room, she pulled the door aside and saw to her relief that Molly was standing facing the wall, running one hand across some scratches in the wood.

"There you are! Molly, can we go now? Peter thinks we should break a window, and I don't know if he's right but there might be another way."

She waited for a reply.

"If there isn't, though," she added, "I suppose breaking the window might be the only choice. And then, I don't know, we can maybe pretend we didn't do it. Our parents might believe that, don't you think?"

Again she waited, but this time she realized that she could hear Molly whispering softly.

"What are you saying?" she asked, before stepping closer. "Molly? You're not being loud enough."

"It was this room," Molly said quietly, still touching the scratches on the wall. "Can't you tell? She kept him in here most of the time."

"I don't know what you're talking about," Charlotte replied.

"He marked the days like this," Molly continued, moving her hand up to a higher part of the wall. "He was trying to keep himself sane over the years and years that he was trapped in here. Sometimes he tried to escape, but after a while he accepted his fate, at least until the end. Meanwhile she fed him and gave him water, I think she was trying to keep him comfortable but..."

Her voice trailed off.

"Who are you talking about?" Charlotte asked.

"You don't know? You should, he was one

of your family. And he was kept here, he chose to be in this place but over time he realized that he was her prisoner."

"I think we should leave," Charlotte told her. "Molly, you're scaring me."

"He tried to end his life," Molly replied. "More than once, he cut his wrists, but she never let him die. He escaped at the end, right at the very end of his life, but only because she allowed him to go. Yes, she *allowed* it, because she knew he was about to die anyway." She traced more of the scratches, some of which formed scraps of words and even – in some places – fragmented sentences. "He wrote over things he'd written previously," she whispered. "It was so sad to see. If he'd just accepted her kindness, he might have lived a long and happy life. Instead he chose to rebel, which was very foolish considering how keen he was to return here originally, after she took him away."

"I still don't know who you're talking about," Charlotte said. "If -"

Suddenly Molly turned and glared at her, with an expression so angry and fixed that Charlotte instinctively took a step back.

"It was all Patience's fault," Molly snarled. "If it hadn't been for Patience, Samuel would have settled much more keenly into his new life here. He would have accepted it all, instead of... Oh, how he moaned and wailed, how he lamented what he'd done to that girl. He worried that by harming her, he'd made her hate him. He said that he had to see her... one... last... time..."

"Molly -"

"And then he warned people to stay away," Molly continued, tilting her head slightly. "Can you believe that? As he lay dying in that horrid public house, he said that no-one else must ever come to this house. Why would he do that? Why would he deny others the chance to be looked after? Just because he was too ungrateful to reap the benefits, he wanted to make sure that no-one else could, although in truth he was really just weak-minded." She took a step toward Charlotte, staring into her eyes. "It was Patience's fault," she sneered. "It was *all* her fault, and she still hasn't paid for her crimes!"

"I don't want to talk to you anymore," Charlotte whimpered, as tears began to roll down her eyes. "Molly, you're starting to scare me."

"But there's still time," Molly sneered, reaching out and placing a hand on Charlotte's shoulder and then squeezing hard. "Do you realize that? She's so old now, and so pathetic, but that doesn't mean she can't be made to suffer one last time!"

"Molly, I -"

Suddenly, before Charlotte had a chance to say another word, Molly's features squeezed into a furious snarl and her eyes blackened as she opened her mouth and screamed.

CHAPTER ELEVEN

"WHAT DO YOU MEAN?" Anne asked, still kneeling over Patience in the hallway. "How can he be away?"

"I don't know the ins and outs of it," Horace replied, holding his hands up in mock surrender. "All I know is that Mrs. Cartwright told me her husband's out of the village today, so he can't come and take a look at Patience. I really don't see that there's anything else I can do, I went to find the man but it's not my fault if he's off gallivanting around seeing people all over the place."

He paused, watching his wife's face in the hope that he'd see some sign she believed him.

"If you ask me," he added, "he should be more attentive to the needs of the villagers here, rather than chasing a quick profit by going off seeing other people, but that's between him and the Lord so -"

"We need to move her, then," Anne said, getting to her feet and stepping around so that she could take hold of Patience's shoulders. "She can't remain here on the floor, Horace. Help me move her into the other room."

"But -"

"Help me, Horace!" she snapped angrily, as Patience let out another faint moan. "For the love of God, will you not just help me this once?"

"Fine," he replied, making his way over and grabbing Patience's ankles, "but you shouldn't talk to me like that. I'm your husband and I demand a little more respect."

"Lift her up."

Looking down at Patience's face, Horace saw for the first time that she was badly bruised from her fall. The old woman's eyes opened momentarily and she stared straight up at him, but she could manage only another low groan before her eyes slipped shut again.

"Horace!" Anne hissed.

"Fine," he said, adjusting his grip on Patience's ankles before lifting them up. "I'm not a cart horse, though. You should think about how you talk to me!"

"Be careful with her," Anne said as they carried Patience through to the next room and laid her on one of the long chairs. "Horace, be gentle! She's old!"

"She's tough, though," he said under his breath. "Evidently she can survive a pretty nasty tumble."

"I need some blankets for her," Anne replied, stepping back and wiping sweat from her brow. "Horace, can you go into the storeroom at the back of the main stable and see what you can find?"

"I wouldn't know where to look."

"I just told you!"

"I don't know about any of that business," he replied, calculating that he only needed a few minutes alone with Patience. "Blankets are a woman's work, anyway. Why don't *you* go and find them, and then bring them back? I'm sure I'd only get it wrong, anyway."

"Sometimes," she said, turning and hurrying to the door, "you are the most infuriating man I could ever possibly imagine."

"That's no way to talk to your husband!" he called after her, before hearing the back door swing open as she hurried outside. "Well," he added, turning back to Patience, "I suppose we'll talk about that later."

He watched as Patience's eyes slipped open again.

"Once we're rich," he added, reaching into his pocket and slowly pulling out the knife he'd fetched from one of the benches. "I'm sorry, Patience," he continued, "I tried to make this quick and easy for you. Why do you cling so keenly to life in this manner, eh? Who does it benefit? Certainly not me, and not Anne, and I daresay not you either. This whole situation is becoming a mess, and I fear I am the only one who can set it straight." He moved the knife toward the old woman's throat. "I shall be quick, I promise. In return, would you mind not struggling too much? Let's make this easy on each other, shall we?"

He began to press the blade against her throat, only for Patience to reach up and grab his wrist, holding him back a little.

"What's this?" he asked. "Are you struggling with me? Patience, dear Patience, the end is here for you. You must see that, you're far too old to be useful to anyone."

She opened her mouth and managed a murmured groan.

"This could already be over," Horace told her, pushing down a little harder with the knife, only for Patience to push back with surprising force. "You're being irritating now," he snarled. "Can't you try to see this whole thing from my point of view? Why are you being so selfish?"

Again Patience pushed back, trying to force the knife away from her throat. Horace looked over his shoulder, just to make sure that Anne wasn't on her way back yet, and then as he looked back down at Patience he placed his other hand on the knife and began to push again.

"You've cheated death once," he said firmly, "but you won't be doing it again. Just try, in your final moments, to remember that your death will bring the rest of us so much happiness. We'll sell that horrible house and it'll be enjoyed by a proper family, and with the money we'll all be able to become better people. I for one was never supposed to be scrambling around in the mud to make a living, I was always destined for better things and now I finally get a chance to prove that!"

He pressed the knife against her throat, and this time her trembling hands weren't strong enough to stop him.

"Goodbye, Patience," he added with just the trace of a smile. "You must see that this is the best outcome for everyone! There's no -"

"Horace?"

Startled, he pulled away from Patience and turned to look at the door, where he saw to his horror that Anne was standing with a bundle of blankets in her arms.

"What are you doing?" she stammered, staring at the knife in his hand as Patience let out a faint wailing sound. "Horace, what were you doing to my grandmother?"

"Nothing!" he replied, trying not to panic as

he got to his feet. "We were just talking, that's all."

He began to make his way over to his wife.

"Oh, are you wondering about the knife?" he asked, holding it up for her to see. "I just have that with me because I'm about to go and strip some leather. You're always complaining that I don't do enough work around the place, aren't you?" He held the knife up for her to see, even as he realized that he was starting to sweat profusely. "There's no time like the present, is there?"

"You had it pressed against her throat," Anne said cautiously.

"Did I?" He paused again, still trying to think of some way to spin events in his own favor. "No, I don't think I did."

"You did, Horace."

"No." He shook his head. "Absolutely not. You've got that all wrong, you're imagining things."

"No, Horace," she replied, watching him with a growing sense of concern, "you were pushing it against her throat and she was trying to push you back. And you were talking to her, you were threatening her and saying goodbye to her."

"That?" He wiped some sweat from his brow. "That was just a little joke."

"It didn't look like a joke," she replied, clearly still worried.

"Well, it was!" he snapped. "It's not my fault if you came in at the end and missed half of it, obviously there's context that you completely missed."

"Horace, why were you threatening my grandmother with a knife?"

"You're just a woman," he told her. "You wouldn't understand. Now why -"

"It's the house, isn't it?" she continued. "You think that with my grandmother gone, you'd be able to persuade me to sell Hadlow House."

"No, I -"

"That's exactly it," she said, taking a step back from him. "I've long known that you're a bit of a rogue, Horace Smudge, but I never had you down as a murderer. Do you honestly think that you can manipulate our family so easily? Are you so foolish as to believe that you'd get away with it?"

"Be careful, Anne," he replied, hoping now that he might be able to intimidate her into submission. "You're saying things that you can't easily take back, and I would remind you that as your husband I am in charge of this household." He took a moment to clear his throat. "I think the best thing would be for you to leave those blankets here so that I can look after poor Patience, while you go and get on with some tasks in the kitchen and think things through."

"Horace..."

"Woman, go!" he snarled, stepping toward her. "I won't tell you again!"

"I'm not leaving you alone with her," Anne told him, looking down at the knife again. "I don't trust you."

"You don't trust me?" he replied, his voice filled with a sense of shock. "Are you serious? I'm your husband and I demand a lot more respect in my own home!" He shoved her hard, forcing her back against the wall. "It's time for you to remember exactly who you're talking to! Go to the kitchen at once, and I shall come through later and remind you of a few important matters and -"

"This isn't your home!" she snapped angrily. "It belongs to *my* family and you had nothing before you married me and moved here! Nothing!" She looked him up and down, as if she was staring at some filthy animal. "You're pathetic, Horace Smudge," she continued breathlessly, "and I should never have married you! Everyone warned me, but I thought you were at least going to be a reliable husband. Now I see that you're nothing short of a common murderer!"

She turned to hurry over to Patience, but at the last second Horace grabbed her and pulled her back. As the blankets fell from her arms, she tried to slip away, only for Horace to pull her again. He stepped closer and tripped slightly, falling forward, and as he steadied himself the knife slid into one side of Anne's belly. Letting out a cry of pain, she pulled back against the wall, but blood was already spreading out across the front of her dress.

"What have you done?" she gasped.

"I'm sorry!" he replied, clearly shocked as he continued to hold the knife in his trembling right hand. "I didn't mean to!"

"Help me!" she replied, putting a hand over the wound. "I need help! I need to find someone!"

She turned to hurry out of the room, only for Horace to grab her again, holding her back once more.

"That isn't going to happen," he said firmly.

"Horace -"

Suddenly he stabbed her again, this time in the center of the belly. He quickly pulled the knife out, and then – seized by the realization that course of action was now set – he told himself that he only had once choice: he stabbed Anne again, this time in the chest, then again and again, attacking her with increasing ferocity and not stopping even as her knees buckled and she began to fall. Holding her up, he continued to stab her until he'd punctured her belly and chest twenty, then thirty, then forty and finally fifty times. As blood erupted from her mouth and she tried to cry out, he merely continued his attack until eventually he moved up to her neck and stabbed her several times in the throat. Only now, as her blood splattered against his face, did he pull back, and he watched as she slithered down to the floor.

"Horace," she groaned, rolling on to her back and staring up at him with a horrified expression, "what..."

In that moment she fell silent, and Horace Smudge – covered in blood – watched calmly as the life faded from his wife's eyes and she let out her final breath.

CHAPTER TWELVE

"WHAT HAPPENED? ARE YOU alright?"

Racing up the stairs, Peter stumbled on a loose floorboard as he hurried into one of the bedrooms just in time for Charlotte to slam against him. As he put his hands on the sides of her arms to hold her in place, he looked past the door and saw Molly grinning at him with a deranged, leery grin.

"Molly?" he said cautiously. "Was that you who screamed just now? What's happening up here?"

"Something just happened," Molly replied, furrowing her brow a little. "That wretched family is done a member. The little girl who hid in here all those years ago..."

She paused, as if she was thinking of something else entirely, something that had happened a long time ago. After a few more seconds the grin on her face grew wider still.

"Yet Patience still lives," she continued. "That's all for the better, since I would deal with her myself, but the other ones can kill among themselves."

"You don't sound like yourself," Peter told her.

"She screamed," Charlotte sobbed. "Peter, she's been saying all sorts of strange things that I don't understand at all! It's almost as if she isn't even Molly at all!"

"Then who would I be?" Molly asked, raising an amused eyebrow. "Answer me that question, young lady. If I am not this wretched, puny little child, then who might I be instead?" She paused for a moment. "And why," she added finally, "have you come uninvited into this place, where you are neither wanted or tolerated?"

"That's not Molly," Charlotte whimpered, pulling away and hiding behind Peter. "It can't be!"

"She's right," Molly replied, keeping her eyes fixed on Peter's face. "Even an idiot can see things clearly from time to time. You have come into this house and you have caused nothing but trouble. Fortunately, while I await other arrivals, I have the necessary opportunity to teach you the folly of your ways."

"Why's she talking like that?" Charlotte

asked, as her voice trembled with fear. "Peter, I don't understand!"

"Take the girl out of here, Mr. Marden," Molly said firmly. "I'll get to her after I have taught this simpering young boy a lesson."

Before Charlotte could ask another question, hands grabbed her from behind. Screaming, she tried to pull away, but instead she was quickly dragged from the room, and the last thing she saw – before the door slammed shut – was Peter turning to look at her. Fear was etched into his face, but once the door was shut Charlotte turned and looked up to see that a pale-looking man had taken hold of her by the shoulders. As soon as she saw this man's face, Charlotte knew that he must be dead, and a moment later she spotted what appeared to be gunshot wounds on his chest.

"Leave me alone!" she screamed, breaking free from his grasp and racing to the stairs, then hurrying down so fast that she almost fell.

Slamming against the front door, she reached for the handle, only to quickly find that it was still missing. Next she tried to use her fingertips to prise the door open, but she immediately realized that this wasn't going to work. She turned and began to make her way toward the kitchen, trying not to panic as she tried to work out how she was going to get away and fetch help, but at the last second she spotted movement ahead. Startled, she froze for a moment as she realized that another ghostly figure was standing in the kitchen, and then she instinctively turned and hurried into the nearest room. Spotting a dining table, she ducked down to take cover and then she turned to look through the legs of a wooden chair and for a few seconds she could only watch the doorway.

Slowly, a figure walked past the door. Based on the figure's clothing, Charlotte assumed that this was a man; a moment later he stopped in the doorway, as if he might be about to step into the room. Holding her breath, Charlotte waited and desperately hoped that he would soon pass.

"May the Lord have mercy on your soul," she heard a man's voice whisper, almost as if he was a priest, and then he stepped out of view.

Breathing a sigh of relief, Charlotte told herself that she had to get to the kitchen, but for now she was too scared to move out from beneath the table. At least under the table, she reasoned, no-one could get to her, and she had time to come up with a plan. She waited for a moment, wondering just how many ghosts were present in Hadlow House, and then – sensing movement – she turned and looked over her shoulder.

A moment earlier she'd run into the empty room and had been sure there was no-one else around. Now, however, she saw the legs of a woman at the far end of the table, sitting in one of the chairs. As her eyes widened with horror, Charlotte realized that once again she was not alone.

***

"Molly, what's wrong with you?" Peter asked, backing away across the bedroom until he bumped against the wall. "Why are you looking at me like that?"

"How am I looking at you?" she asked calmly.

"I don't like this," he replied, turning and hurrying to the door, only to find that it was now sealed tight. Even as he pulled on the handle, he knew that it wasn't going to budge. "I want to go home."

"Perhaps you *are* home," she said behind him.

"I don't live here," he pointed out, trying the handle yet again. "You can do what you want, but I want to go home right now!"

"Oh, I know I can do what I want," she told him. "In the confines of this house, when there is no master present, I am in charge. And there has been no master present for many, many years."

He turned to her, and in that moment he felt more certain than ever that it was not truly Molly who stared back at him from those darkened eyes.

"Samuel Butler was so ungrateful," she

continued. "You have no idea how hard I tried to please him, and for how long, but there was always a part of him that wanted to reject my care."

She took a step forward.

"He left his mark on the walls of this house," she added, "so that not a day goes by when I am not faced with evidence of his unhappiness."

"I don't know who you're talking about," he stammered, trying desperately to hide the fact that he was terrified.

"I'm talking about Mr. Samuel Butler," she said, as if this was the most obvious thing in the whole world. "He was the second master I have had at Hadlow House. The less said about the first, the better, but I felt from the beginning that Mr. Butler was made of sterner stuff. That he would take his role more seriously, and that he would control his family properly. I still believe that I was correct, it's just that he was tempted away from the path of righteousness by others. Specifically, by that wretched miscreant of a daughter."

"Why are you talking like this?" he whimpered.

"He used to cry out for her, you know," she continued, taking another step toward him. "All night, sometimes. Patience's name was rarely far from his tongue, especially toward the end of his miserable life. No matter how I tried to adapt to his needs and desires, he just couldn't forget that straggly little girl."

"Charlotte!" Peter shouted, banging on the door. "Help me!"

"She can't save you," Molly told him.

"Charlotte, I can't open the door!" he yelled, still slamming his fists against the wood. "Something's really wrong with Molly and she's scaring me!"

"Does the truth scare you?"

"Leave me alone!" he gasped, turning to her. "I'm not -"

As soon as he saw that she was directly behind him, he froze and stared with horror into her eyes. He desperately wanted to run away, but something about her gaze seemed almost to be forcing him to remain on the spot, until finally he felt as if his knees were about to buckle. The air was getting colder all around, and for a few more seconds he could only look into her eyes as he tried to understand exactly who or what was staring back.

"You're not Molly," he whispered through gritted teeth. "Who are you?"

"I'm just borrowing her body," she replied, tilting her head again as she maintained eye-contact with him. "My name is Mrs. Baxter and I am the housekeeper of this fine home. Although I have not had much to do, not since the departure of poor, dear Mr. Samuel Butler."

AMY CROSS

CHAPTER THIRTEEN

Twenty-five years earlier...

"HELP ME," SAMUEL WHISPERED, his voice cracking under the weight of so many years as he knelt on the bedroom floor and scratched another message into the wooden wall. "Please -"

Before he could finish, the nail of his right thumb broke. Wincing and pulling back, he saw blood dribbling from the nail-bed, and after a moment he reached up and carefully pulled the broken section of nail away. He felt another sharp pain, and then he turned to see the spot on the wall where he'd begun to write his daughter's name.

"Patience," he said under his breath, "what -"

Suddenly feeling a hand on his shoulder, he

spun around and slammed back against the wall. He looked around the gloomy bedroom, but there was no sign of anyone and the only sound came from rain hitting the window and crashing down onto the roof. Before he had time to react, however, he realized that the shadows on the far side of the room was twisting slightly, as if some presence was starting to make itself known, although a few seconds later he heard a floorboard creaking somewhere far off in the house, perhaps at the bottom of the stairs. He turned and looked at the closed door that led out onto the landing.

"Who's there?" he stammered.

"Mr. Butler?"

Although he recognized the man's voice coming from the other side of the closed door, Samuel was unable in that moment to remember precisely where he had heard it before.

"Who is that?" he asked.

"Mr. Butler," the voice replied, "what a terrible thing you have done."

"What are you talking about?" Samuel paused, before crawling toward the door. "I must ask you again, Sir, who are you?"

"I came to your home with the best of intentions," the voice said, "and you repaid me with brutality and unkindness."

"I don't remember..."

"Come now," the voice said, "it was not so

long ago, though admittedly you are an old man now. Far older than I was ever permitted to become."

"I don't know who you are," Samuel told him, "or if -"

In that moment, a sudden burst of realization hit his thoughts and he pulled back a little from the door.

"Father... Father Ward?" he said cautiously. "But how is this possible? I saw... I saw you..."

His voice trailed off.

"Did you think any good would come from this, Mr. Butler?" Father Ward replied. "Do you believe that I should pray for your soul at all?"

"I -"

"What did you do to that poor girl, Mr. Butler?" the priest asked. "What did you do to your poor, dear daughter Patience?"

"I thought I had to," Samuel sobbed, as tears filled his eyes. "I thought I had to come back to the house at any cost, and -"

Hearing a bumping sound, he looked over his shoulder. He knew that he wasn't truly alone in the room, but after a few seconds he realized that at least the ghostly figure was not showing herself just yet; turning to the door again, he thought back to that awful day in the village when he'd driven a knife into his daughter's belly.

"Tell me," he continued, "does she yet live?

This is the one thing I must know before I... before I go to my judgment. Did Patience survive what I did to her?"

"I would not know that, Sir," Father Ward replied. "I am trapped here, albeit not in the same way that *you* are trapped. If the girl lived, she would be a woman now, perhaps a mother herself. But do you really think that she would want to see you? Do you really think that you could ever be forgiven?"

"I just want to know that she is alright," Samuel sobbed. "That I did not... snuff out her life."

He hesitated, horrified by the memory of that awful moment, which was now replaying over and over in his mind. Indeed, he was so stricken by this thought that he did not initially hear the slow click of the door starting to open, and he only noticed when the door's edge bumped against his shoulder. Shocked, he pulled back, only for the door – which had remained shut for so very long – to finally swing all the way open, revealing the landing and the top of the stairs.

"Father Ward?" he whispered cautiously, seeing no sign of anyone out there. "Are you still here?"

"You are of no further use to me," the woman's voice sneered from behind him. "You are so old now. I don't know what's more pathetic, the marks you have made on the wall or the marks you have made on your own flesh."

"Help me," he replied, half-turning before he caught his own reflection in the window, mixed with the rain dribbling down the other side. For a moment he was shocked by the sight of such an old, thin man. "How long have I spent trapped in this infernal house?"

"You came back of your own volition," she replied. "You must remember that. Now you can leave."

He opened his mouth to reply, before hearing a creaking sound coming from the landing. Turning again, he was horrified by the sight of his own dead wife hanging from a rope above the stairs.

"But I want something from you," the voice behind him continued, as a cold dead hand rested on his shoulder. "Find Patience. You will be pleased to know that she still lives. Find her and tell her that I am waiting for her."

***

Rain coursed down the country lane that led into Cobblefield, creating a slippery path that had almost brought Samuel down several times. Clutching the low stone wall for support, he saw the village spread out ahead and realized that finally his long walk from the house was almost over.

Two men were loading boxes onto the back of some kind of carriage, getting on with their work even in the terrible conditions. Samuel immediately tried to call out to them, but he could barely raise his voice above a pitiful moan so he let go of the wall and tried his best to walk toward them instead. He knew that he might fall at any moment, that his legs were barely keeping him upright, but he told himself that somewhere in the village his daughter Patience was waiting, and that he was finally going to get one last chance to see her, so that he could tell her he was sorry and warn her to stay away from that wretched house forever.

"Please," he stammered, "where is she? Where is my -"

Suddenly he tripped, slamming down hard against the road. He immediately tried to get up, but he found that he was too weak. As more and more rain crashed down, soaking him still further, he heard voices moving closer and when he looked up he was able – just about – to make out two figures standing over him. They were the two men from the carriage, and he felt a rush of relief as he realized that he had at last been noticed.

"Who is this?" one of the men asked. "I don't recognize him."

"Neither do I," the other man replied, before crouching down. "Sir! You there, are you from round here? Why are you out in such awful weather? Haven't you heard that this storm is liable to get worse before it gets better?"

Samuel managed little more than a faint groan. He had made it so far, he was at the edge of the village now, but he could feel his body starting to fail. Death was close, yet he knew that he had to see Patience first, that he would fight against his own dwindling mortality if necessary. He tried again to speak, but his throat began to seize and he felt as if he might never get another word out again.

"How old is this poor bastard?" one of the men said. "I'd wager he's almost a hundred!"

"I'd wager that you're right," the other man replied. "Yet there is something about him that I recognize."

"You think you've seen him before?"

"No," the second man said, seemingly lost in thought for a moment, "it is more that he reminds me of someone. His eyes, do they not seem somehow familiar to you?"

Worried that he might pass out and never wake up again, Samuel knew in that moment that he had to find some last scrap of strength. Patience was nearby, he felt sure of that, and he realized that he had to warn her never to go anywhere near Hadlow House again. Even if he himself was condemned to spend the rest of eternity in the fires of Hell, he knew he could do so only if he was sure that his daughter had been saved. Finally he reached out to one of the men, grabbing his arm and squeezing as hard as he could manage in one last attempt to find a little strength.

"Where is she?" he stammered, as rain ran down his face. "Please... where is Patience?"

CHAPTER FOURTEEN

Twenty-five years later...

"I DON'T KNOW WHO Samuel Butler is," Peter said, his voice quaking with fear. "Please, I don't know anything about anyone. I just want to leave this house and never come back."

"He once stood where you're standing now," Molly replied, stepping closer still and reaching out to touch his arm. "He too wanted to leave, and eventually I granted him his wish, yet how did he repay me? He did not send Patience here. Instead, he warned her to stay away, and that she has done ever since."

"I don't know what -"

"I saw her once," she continued, cutting him off as she gripped his arm tighter and tighter. "After her husband's untimely death, I saw her from the window but she did not dare to come inside. How is that possible? How can she be such a coward?"

"You're hurting me!" he gasped, trying but failing to pull his arm away. "Molly, please, let go!"

"I thought that would teach her a lesson," she snarled. "Don't you think that it should have done? She should have realized on that night that she could never truly deny me, yet still she ran and then she left this place deserted. I have had nobody for company except a handful of foolish ghosts, and I have found them to offer very limited entertainment."

"Stop!" Peter hissed, trying again and again to get his arm free as he felt her fingernails digging harder and harder into his flesh. "Molly, let go of me or I'm going to -"

Suddenly he lost his footing and fell, landing with a thud against the floor. At the same time his arm jerked free from Molly's grasp, but when he looked at the scratches he immediately saw blood running from the wounds.

"I thought you were going to break it!" he cried out, struggling to hold back tears as he began to sit up. "I thought -"

Before he could finish, Molly grabbed the top of his head and shoved it back, slamming the back against the door and then holding him in position as she glared down into his eyes.

"Molly!" he yelled. "Stop!"

"My name is not Molly," she sneered, "and I have had many years to contemplate what I should have done to Samuel Butler before he left this house. I was perhaps too kind to him back then, but I shall not make the same mistake." She placed her other hand on the side of his face and began to press her thumb against his eyes. "My first two messages to Patience seemingly did not get through. Let us hope that the third time proves luckier."

She pressed harder, until the nail of her right thumb began to cut into the white of Peter's eyeball, and all he could do in response was scream.

***

A scream rang out, filling the entire house with such force that Charlotte immediately looked up toward the underside of the table.

Having been hidden away for a couple of minutes now, staring in horror at the legs of whoever was sitting at the table's far end, she now realized that Peter needed her help. She froze for a few seconds as the scream twisted and curdled, and then – just as she was starting to realize that she had to make a decision – she heard the cry end abruptly before glass shattered somewhere upstairs.

A moment later she heard an ominous thud hitting the ground outside, as if something or someone had been thrown from one of the windows.

"Peter?" she whispered, hoping against hope that he would suddenly call out to tell her that everything was fine. "Peter, are you there?"

She waited, and after a few seconds she heard a rustling sound coming from somewhere outside the house. She furrowed her brow as she listened, and now she couldn't shake the feeling that somebody was out there, although after a few seconds any hint of footsteps began to stumble away.

"Peter?" she called out again, trying once more not to panic. "Can you hear me? Peter, I'm down here!"

Again she waited, but the house remained silent. After a few seconds, realizing that she couldn't simply hide under the table forever, she began to crawl out.

"Don't go to her," a woman's voice said softly.

Charlotte froze immediately. She knew that this was the voice of the woman in the chair, but she also knew that the woman in the chair shouldn't be there at all.

"Everything that is bad about this house is because of her," the voice continued. "Even poor Catherine could have had her peace, if Fanny had not interfered."

Slowly, Charlotte turned and looked back toward the legs.

"And my dear Richard might have stood a chance," the voice explained, "if it hadn't been for that vain, calculating shrew and her machinations. Every soul trapped in this house owes their misery to Fanny Baxter one way or another, and she's not done yet. The only lucky ones are those who died here and have not been forced to remain, for they at least have escaped her in death."

"Who... who are you?" Charlotte whispered.

"Once you are here," the woman replied, "I fear you cannot leave unless she wants you gone. There was the girl who many years ago escaped by climbing the chimney, but no-one else has ever been able to go, not until Fanny agrees."

"Can you help me?" Charlotte asked. "My friend Molly is acting really strangely and I just want to go home."

"Then you must beg Fanny for permission."

"I don't know who Fanny is," Charlotte replied.

She waited for an answer, but now the house had fallen silent again. A moment later, however, she flinched and looked over her shoulder as she heard footsteps making their way out from one of the upstairs bedrooms and onto the landing.

"Who's Fanny?" she asked again, with a growing sense of panic.

"I fear she has taken your little friend as her own," the voice explained. "That is not something she has done before, but let nobody ever say that Fanny Baxter is not enterprising. She will do whatever is in her power to get what she wants, and what she wants is to run this house."

Before she could reply, Charlotte heard somebody slowly but surely starting to make their way down the staircase.

"Please just help me get out of here," she whimpered, pulling back a little from the door while taking care to not get too close to the legs. "It's not my fault that we came to the house, I didn't even want to!"

"That won't help you now."

"But -"

"Nothing can help any of us now. We are trapped here, most of us are dead but you are alive." She paused. "For now."

"I just want to go home," Charlotte wept as she spotted a shadow moving in the hallway. Whoever was on the stairs, they were almost at the bottom now. "Why can't I go home?"

"I too would like to go home," the voice continued. "I am sure my father is long dead, but I would give anything to see London again. At first I was waiting for my husband to come for me, but I understand now that he is dead and gone. It seems now that I must simply sit here and..."

She paused for a few more seconds.

"I feel them in my head," she added. "Wriggling. Squirming. Sometimes they infect my thoughts and make me want to chew the rotten wood on the window-frames, or long for the dirty mud of the riverbed. I used to try to fight them, but now I see them as my only friends. At least they mean that I am not alone here. No matter how quiet the house gets sometimes – and it can be *very* quiet when all the ghosts are resting – I can always hear them burrowing through my mind."

"I don't understand," Charlotte whimpered, "but -"

Suddenly hearing a floorboard creaking out in the hallway, she turned and looked at the door. The shadow was moving across the opposite wall now, and a moment later Molly stepped into view, even though Charlotte could only see the lower half of her body from under the table.

"Hello, Charlotte," Molly said, her voice sounding much darker and angrier than usual. "Your little friend has had to leave, I needed him to deliver a message to the village for me. But you..."

She hesitated, before stepping into the dining room.

"You," she continued, "are far more important. Because you are part of that awful family. You are Patience's kin, and for that you must pay a very high price indeed."

CHAPTER FIFTEEN

SLOWLY, HORACE LEANED FORWARD and looked down into Anne's dead, vacant eyes. He waited, fully aware that he'd been wrong about Patience earlier, but somehow this time he knew for sure.

His wife was dead.

Looking at the front of her torso, he saw that blood had soaked her clothes and was now pooling on the floor. He reached out to touch the fabric, but he pulled his hand away as soon as he felt something wet on his fingertips; he turned his hand around and saw the little dabs of blood, and then he withdrew and bumped his back against the wall before slithering down onto the floor.

Over on the chair, Patience let out a pained groan.

Horace opened his mouth, but for a few seconds longer he could only stare at his wife's bloodied corpse. Despite the huge amount of blood that she had lost, there was still a part of him that wondered whether she would managed a sudden gasp or twitch, some little sign that she was alive. As the seconds passed, however, he began to truly understand that she was gone, and he felt a growing sense of rage starting to rise up through his chest until finally seven words slipped from his lips.

"Why did you do this to me?"

He gave her a chance to answer, even though he knew she would never answer again.

"Why?" he barked angrily. "Anne, why did you have to nag and doubt me so much? I'm your husband, why couldn't you simply accept my decisions?"

Taking a deep breath, he felt as if he was on the verge of breaking into great peals of laughter.

"None of this had to happen," he chuckled. "You realize that, don't you? I was right all along, and this horrible tragedy only proves that fact. I told you what we should do, but were you willing to listen? Of course not." Sighing, he shook his head as he sat up a little. "You poor, deluded woman," he continued, "look what you've done to yourself. You always had a stubborn streak in you, I admit that, but I truly never thought that it would lead you to such an awful end."

Getting to his feet, he held up the blood-smeared knife in his right hand and shook his head with a growing sense of disbelief.

"Why did you make this happen?" he asked. "I swear, as long as I live I shall never understand the female mind."

He hesitated, before stepping over to her and looking down at her pale dead face. After a moment he turned the knife so that the blade was pointing at her, and he made a series of jabbing motions in the air.

"You should have agreed to sell the house when I first pointed out that it was a good idea," he told her. "Why did you have to argue back all the time? Why were you so greedy that you felt you had to keep the house and all its value locked away for yourself, eh? Did you have no self-awareness at all?"

Hearing another groan coming from the other side of the room, he turned and looked over at Patience.

"You know this was all her fault, don't you?" he shouted, before making his way toward her and stopping to watch as she tried in vain to sit up. "All I wanted," he continued, "was to help my family get a better life. I wanted to sell that miserable pile of bricks to anyone who wants to live there or tear it down. I don't care what happens to the place, but if you think I'm happy to spend the rest of my life rotting in some yard in Cobblefield, then you really don't understand human nature at all." He waved the knife in her face. "I'm getting out of here, and I'm sorry that Anne couldn't see the potential, but that's not my fault at all. She was in my way, and I'm afraid you are too, so..."

He paused, watching her throat and imagining the knife slicing through her skin, but after a moment he managed to hold himself back.

"I might need you," he muttered, clearly annoyed by the realization. "Just for now, just for legal things like signing papers, I might need you alive, but only until I've managed to arrange things with Mr. Wadsworth. Now that Anne's gone, you might have bought yourself a little time, but not much." He waited for a response, but in truth he wasn't even sure that Patience could hear him at all; she seemed lost in her own little world. "First I need to dispose of the evidence," he added, nodding gently. "Yes, I need to make sure that no-one starts asking too many questions. You're going to have to wait here, Patience. Don't worry, though. I won't be long."

***

"A little lye," Horace muttered a short while later, as he stood at the edge of one of the fields on the outskirts of Cobblefield, "and a few other drops of this and that, and we should be set."

Having almost worn himself out entirely digging a hole on a patch of untended land, he was now pouring various substances into the depths. Snow and ice had slowed him down, and he was already soaked to the skin, but a kind of fervor had overtaken his senses and all he could think was that he needed to get Anne's body buried as quickly as possible. As the various noxious liquids splattered into the pit, Horace continually glanced around to make sure that he wasn't about to be spotted, even though he knew that no-one in their right mind would be out on such a wretched day. He could see Cobblefield about a mile back to the north, and in every other direction there was nothing but the rolling English countryside.

Finally, having emptied the jugs, he set them down and made his way over to the cart. The horse whinnied and turned to watch, as if it knew that it was witnessing something that shouldn't be occurring.

"Don't judge me," Horace replied, fully aware that he was being watched. "You don't know what it's like. I've been denied that money for so long!"

Hauling Anne's body onto his shoulders, he turned and carried her toward the makeshift grave. As soon as he was at the edge he let her tumble down, and he heard a crunch as she slammed into the depths of the pit. Already a little out of breath, Horace nevertheless immediately grabbed the shovel and began to push dirt back into the grave, determined to swiftly cover up any evidence of his crime.

"She went to visit her sister," he muttered as he rehearsed some possible explanations for his wife's disappearance. "Wait, she doesn't have a sister. She went to visit a sick friend. Who?"

Stopping for a moment as his arms burned with pain, he tried to think of a more plausible story. On the way out to the field he'd assumed that it would be easy enough to explain Anne's sudden departure, but now he found himself worrying that snooping locals might yet start asking too many questions.

"She's sick, is what she is," he murmured finally, under his breath, as snow continued to fall all around. He looked into the grave and saw that while Anne's body was still wrapped in the old sack he'd taken from the stable, one of her hands had slipped out and was now settled against the mud. He saw her bloodied, curled fingers and felt a shiver run through his bones. "She's sick and she's gone off to get well," he continued. "No, I don't know how long she'll be. I think the girl and I might have to go and be with her. That's the only thing for it."

He paused, and in that moment he thought that maybe – just maybe – one of Anne's fingers moved slightly. He told himself that this was merely a trick of the light, and that explanation might very well have been true, but a moment later he began to shovel dirt into the grave with ever-increasing intensity, keen to get the body buried as fast as possible.

Just in case.

"She was dead, alright," he told himself, and now Anne could no longer be seen at all. "No-one could have survived all of that... unpleasantness that she brought upon her own poor body."

Still he shoveled, pushing through the pain until finally he'd managed to fill the grave. Stepping back, he leaned against the shovel for a moment as he admired his handiwork, and he realized that soon snow would cover the grave entirely and that would be the end of the matter. Eventually the snow would thaw, of course, but by then the soil would have healed itself and there would be no sign that Anne had ever even existed. She was gone, and that was all that he cared about.

"I'll miss you," he said, briefly and scruffily making the sign of the cross against his chest, before turning and heading back to the horse and cart. "It's not my fault you made me do this, though. I'm just an honest man trying to make his honest way through life."

CHAPTER SIXTEEN

"I KNOW YOU'RE THERE," Molly's voice said after a moment's silence, her tone seeming to somehow scratch the very air that hung in the house's cold dining room. "Are you really determined to play this foolish game?"

Still hiding under the table, Charlotte pulled back a little. After a moment, remembering the woman at the other end of the table, she turned to make sure that she wasn't about to bump into the legs sitting in the chair; she immediately saw, however, that the chair was now empty, as if the strange woman had faded to nothing as soon as Molly had entered the room.

Suddenly hearing a tapping sound, Charlotte turned and saw that a small stone had fallen onto the floor at Molly's feet. This was followed by another, then another, and Charlotte already felt that she had seen these stones before.

"So strange," Molly continued, "that he had collected these things in his little cloth bag. Whatever is the point of them."

She let several more of Peter's stones hit the floor, and then she gently kicked them aside with the shoe on her right foot.

"Charlotte Purkiss," she said, her voice quaking with rage, "or... is that the right name? No, because your mother married, did she not? You are... Charlotte Smudge."

Charlotte opened her mouth to reply, but her body was tense with fear now.

"You are not even related to Patience by blood, are you?" Molly continued, as she started to slowly walk around the table. Frozen in place, Charlotte was just about able to turn and watch her progress. "Your mother is... *was* Anne, and she was the granddaughter of poor Daniel who made the mistake of returning to this house. So unless I am very much mistaken, you do not share any of Patience's blood, but that does not make you any less a part of her family."

She stopped next to the chair in which – until a few moments earlier – the other woman had been sitting.

"You are still," Molly added, "a thing I can use to make her hurt."

Another tear ran down Charlotte's cheek.

"I could have pulled this table aside by now, you now," Molly explained. "I could have been far more forceful than I have been so far, yet I have chosen to let you make the right choice. Do you think you can do that, Charlotte? Do you think you can crawl out and face me properly, woman to woman?"

"Help!" Charlotte screamed, turning and looking back through to the hallway. "Peter, I'm in here!"

"Peter is gone," Molly said calmly.

"Somebody help me!" Charlotte sobbed, before breaking down again. "Peter wouldn't go," she whimpered. "He wouldn't just leave me here like this."

"He had little say in the matter," Molly explained. "Besides, you came and hid down here, did you not? I am unaware of you having made any great attempt to rush back up and help him."

She stepped around the table again, making her way past the window.

"Patience would have tried something," she continued. "Oh, might she have climbed up the chimney again?"

"Help!" Charlotte shouted, slamming her fists angrily against the floorboards.

"She would have made the effort, at least," Molly said. "She always tried to do the right thing, in the end. But you, Charlotte, are only tinged by Patience's qualities. You remind me a little, too, of your mother Anne. She came to visit me once. She hid in a cupboard, which was mildly more enterprising than taking refuge beneath a table. She had some fight in her too, but you..."

She stopped again, and now her feet were only a few inches from Charlotte's hands.

"You have qualities of your father," she continued. "I can see it now. His name is Horace, is it not? He's the local drunk. Obviously you're not a drunk, Charlotte, not yet, but you have his qualities of cowardice and selfishness."

"No, I don't!" Charlotte shouted.

"Those are big words, coming from a girl hiding beneath a table."

Hearing the sound of fingernails scratching against the table's top, Charlotte looked up. She could see the table's underside, and she knew full well that Molly's hand was moving across the upper side of the wood, as if she was trying to scratch her way through.

"Peter, you have to come and help me," Charlotte sobbed. "Don't leave me here! Peter, please!"

"You won't get any aid from that direction," Molly said firmly. "I'm afraid that young Peter is... otherwise occupied."

***

"There he is," Alice Nichols said as she stood outside the church in Cobblefield, watching a horse and cart on the horizon, "coming back from wherever he's been. What business would a man like Horace Smudge have out in the fields on a day like this?"

"I would have thought he'd be in the public house by now," Elizabeth Warner replied, furrowing her brow as she watched the distant cart turning onto the narrow road that wound its way into the village from the south. "It's rare to see Horace doing anything useful at all, at any time of the day or night."

"Which is what makes me wonder what he's up to," Alice said. "When a lazy man suddenly bursts into a fit of activity, there's rarely a good cause."

"What are you suggesting?" Elizabeth asked with a faint smile. "That Horace is up to his old tricks?"

"Only that I would not trust that man as far as I could throw him," Alice explained, "and that I am eternally glad he is not *my* husband. I certainly would never have consented to marry such a wretch. I sometimes wonder what made poor Anne Purkiss fall for him."

"Perhaps it was his striking good looks,"

Elizabeth suggested.

Both women paused, before starting to laugh as more and more snow fell all around them. And then, hearing a shuffling sound, they both turned and looked along the road behind them, and they saw to their surprise that a young boy was stumbling away from the pass that led into the forest.

"Is that little Peter Finch?" Elizabeth asked, recognizing the boy even though his head was bowed. "Why is he walking like that?"

Barely able to stay upright on two twisted legs, Peter stumbled and almost fell. He was clutching something dark and red in his hands, and as he got closer Elizabeth saw that this was some kind of stained cloth bag.

"Peter Finch, what are you doing?" she called out. "Peter, your mother has been searching for you, she was out of her mind with worry! Where have you been?"

She waited, and then she stepped before him. As if he hadn't even noticed her, Peter almost walked straight into her arms, and he only stopped when she reached out and placed a hand against his shoulder. Still keeping his head bowed, he held the blood-soaked cloth bag in his shaking hands.

"Peter," Elizabeth said cautiously, "what is the matter? I want you to look at me right now. Do you understand?"

She waited, before glancing back at Alice, who shared her expression of concern.

"Now, Peter," Elizabeth continued, turning to the boy again and feeling a growing sense of fear as she looked at the bag, "this is very ungentlemanly behavior. Do you realize that? I know your mother rather well, and I am sure she has taught you how to properly address a lady. You should bid me good afternoon and ask me how my day is going, and then you should hurry on while causing as little nuisance as possible."

"Peter Finch," Alice barked, making her way over and stopping next to Elizabeth, "this is really a very poor show. Cobblefield might only be a small village, but we should still remember our manners."

"What is in that bag?" Elizabeth asked, before reaching out and slowly taking the bag from his hands. "Why, it's absolutely soaked with blood, Peter. What have you been doing?"

"I don't like this," Alice murmured, taking a step back. "Have you been killing innocent little birds, Peter? That's really not the done thing!"

"What is in here?" Elizabeth asked again. Her hands were trembling, but she began to open the bag, only for its contents to tumble out into the palm of her hand. "What -"

Gasping with shock, she saw two bloodied, partially torn eyeballs, complete with damaged nerves trailing at the back. A large, bloodier piece of meat had fallen out as well, ripped at one end, and Elizabeth saw to her horror that this appeared to be a tongue. Then, before she could react further, another chunk of meat rolled out onto her hand and she found herself holding a human nose, followed a moment later by two curled sections of flesh that resembled ears. And then, as she looked at Peter, the young boy raised his head so that his face was now revealed, with his eyes gouged out and almost all his distinguishing features having been ripped away.

Letting out a pained gurgle, as if he was trying to speak, Peter could only manage a brief groan before a torrent of dark blood began to gush from his mouth.

CHAPTER SEVENTEEN

"GET HIM IN HERE!" Doctor Cartwright called out, gesturing for the men to follow him through to the room at the rear of his home. "Hurry!"

"This isn't right," Arthur Barlow said, his voice tight with fear as he led the others, who were carrying Peter between them. "So help me, it's like something from the pits of Hell."

"The two women are in the front room with your wife," Nathaniel Jones explained as he and two others took Peter to the table and set him down. "They both fainted, but are being revived now."

"Let me see the child," Cartwright replied, slipping between them and approaching the table. "There might yet be -"

Before he could finish, he saw the full extent of the damage to Peter's face. Even for a man with so much experience, Cartwright was still stopped in his tracks as he looked into the bloodied, pulped eye sockets and then looked down to see part of the boy's skull exposed through the meat where he had once had a nose. A moment later the boy's mouth hung open, revealing the taped stump of what had once been his tongue.

"Doctor?" Thomas Crowther said, standing on the other side of the table and staring in horror at what was left of the poor boy's features. "Can anything be done for him?" He hesitated, before placing the bloodied bag down, revealing the eyeballs and assorted other facial features that had been saved. "He had these with him, or so the women claimed. I don't know, they seemed rather hysterical, but they swore that he was carrying this bag when he first arrived back in the village."

"I..."

For a few seconds, Cartwright seemed too stunned to know what to do. He looked at the eyeballs, and then at the boy, and then – hearing footsteps – he turned and saw Peter's parents Eleanor and John rushing into the room.

"Is it true?" Eleanor gasped, hurrying around to look into her son's face. "They said -"

As soon as she saw the horror of his injuries, she let out an agonized scream and pulled back. After just a fraction of a second her scream ended and she fainted, while her husband John stopped and stared in silent disbelief as Peter reached out with his hands to try to find his mother.

"I think I might go and try to find Father Walker," Thomas Crowther muttered, turning and heading toward the door. "It's at a time like this that I need a little... spiritual guidance. I need someone to explain to me how such horrors are able to exist in the world."

"What do we do, Doctor Cartwright?" Arthur Barlow asked. "Please, tell us that you can put the boy back to how he was!"

"I cannot," Cartwright replied, shaking his head slowly as the first tears reached his eyes. "That task is beyond the skill of any man. I fear that the only thing to be done is..." He paused, before turning to John. "May the Lord have mercy on my soul," he continued, "but is there any kindness in even allowing the child to live like this?"

***

"It's that house," Arthur Barlow said darkly, as he stood at the bar in *The Shoemaker* and stared down at his drink. Having hurried to the church, he'd made a brief detour into the public house. "I'll bet you anything in the world that the boy has been to that house."

"You don't know it for sure, though," replied Jack Keats, the landlord as he stood on the other side of the bar. "We should wait to hear from the boy's own mouth what -"

"His tongue was cut out!" Arthur said angrily. "You'll never hear anything from his mouth ever again, not now!"

"I admit that it sounds bad," Jack murmured, as a few other men entered the pub, "but there's absolutely no sense in marching off based on assumptions. What would you even do, anyway? No-one has been living in Hadlow House for many a year."

"But it's still there!" Arthur hissed. "Don't you get it? For as long as that house is standing out there, its evil will find a way to snake into this village and cause us harm!"

"Now you sound paranoid," Jack said as he began to pour drinks for the new arrivals. "Don't get me wrong, I'm no fan of that house at all, but it's just bricks and mortar. You can't seriously believe all those foolish tales about there being something else out there." He watched Arthur, waiting for a reply. "Can you?"

"I believe what I see with my own two eyes," Arthur told him, "and that's that poor little Peter Finch..." He paused as he thought back to the horrific sight. "He barely even seemed human," he continued, feeling as if his blood was on the verge of running cold. "It was like something evil had ripped off everything that made him look like a person, and had left nothing but blood and meat. I even saw part of his skull showing through, as if death itself was slowly bursting from beneath his young skin. And I'm telling you, as God is my witness, that no man could do that to a child. Whatever did that to him... it must be pure and undiluted evil of the highest order."

He turned to see that everyone in the room was now listening to him.

"And it lives in that house!" he spat at them.

"I'm not sure that it *lives*," Matthew Wallace suggested.

"That place should have been ripped apart years ago," Arthur continued, "back when those two American traitors holed up at the place. Or even earlier than that, it should have been torn down after what happened to the Butler family. Everyone knows that Hadlow House is cursed, so why will no-one do anything to fix the problem?"

He waited for an answer, but he quickly saw that only blank, somewhat helpless faces were staring back at him.

"Will you leave it to me, then?" he asked. "Must I bear the cross of this task??"

Again he waited, and after a moment – feeling a growing sense of disgust – he got to his feet and downed the last of his beer before heading toward the door.

"I never knew that Cobblefield was the

home of so many cowards," he continued, "but the cowardice of one man has nothing to do with the bravery of another, so I'll take the burden if it is to be mine." He pulled the door open with such force that it slammed against the wall, and then he turned to see that the assembled drinkers were all still watching him. "Is there not one of you who'll come out there with me?" he barked. "Not one man who'll stand up and help make sure that no more of our sons and daughters are harmed by that..."

His voice trailed off for a moment as he struggled to come up with the right word.

"Ghost?" a man by the window suggested, prompting a series of chuckles to spread around the room.

"You don't take it seriously," Arthur snarled. "Fine, that is your choice, but I'm going to make sure that poor young Peter is the very last victim of Hadlow House. And if all the rest of you can do is laugh, then that's fine by me."

"Why don't you come and have another drink?" Jack called after him, but Arthur was already gone and the door swung gently shut with a dull bump.

"He's cracking up," a man at the far end of the bar observed. "He's losing his mind."

"He might have a point," Jack replied.

"But -"

"I remember when old Samuel Butler was

brought in here and laid out on those very tables over there," Jack continued. "My old man ran the pub back then, if he was still here you could ask him what happened. I remember old Mr. Butler's face as if it was yesterday, though. I saw the pain and fear in his eyes, and I heard the terror in his voice. They say he'd been up at Hadlow House for decades, trapped alone in there with God-knows-what for company." He looked around at the other men in the pub and saw that he had their rapt attention. "I'm not saying for sure what's going on there, one way or the other," he added, "but *something* about that house isn't right. And if Arthur Barlow goes and burns it down, and then nothing bad ever happens again, well... I suppose we'll all be able to rest a little easier, even if we don't necessarily find out the truth."

The others began to talk to one another, and Jack rolled his eyes as he realized that the conversation was moving on. He still couldn't help looking at the tables by the window, however, and he thought back to that day many years earlier when those tables had been pushed together so that they could be used as Samuel Butler's deathbed. He made the sign of the cross against his chest, and then he went to serve a regular at the far end of the bar who was ready for another beer.

CHAPTER EIGHTEEN

"THAT'S BETTER," HORACE SNARLED as he pulled the rope tight, making sure that Patience was still firmly held down on the chair in the back room. "We don't want you wandering off again, do we?"

"Where's Daniel?" she whispered, looking all around.

"Oh, you'll be seeing Daniel again soon enough," he told her. "And Anne. And anyone else you fancy. Provided they've already gone ahead, that is." He took a step back. "I just need to get in touch with Mr. Wadsworth and check that I don't need you for anything, and then I'll be more than happy to dispatch you to whatever world might be waiting for you. It's not like there's much point to you being here, anyway. You haven't really been right in the head for years, have you? You're barely even yourself."

"Daniel should be home soon," Patience told him, sounding a little puzzled by her husband's absence. "Yes, I'm sure he'll walk through the door at any moment, and then he can explain exactly what's going on. In the meantime, where are Anne and Charlotte? I would so dearly like to see them and talk for a while."

"They're busy," he replied, turning and ducking his head down as he stepped through into the kitchen.

Spotting a chessboard on the corner table, he wandered over and saw that a game was in progress. He knew that his wife had often played with Patience, and that she had tried to interest Charlotte in the game without any success. As far as he was concerned, the rules were entirely incomprehensible.

"Nothing more than stupidity," he murmured, reaching out to knock the pieces over before hearing a knock on the door at the front of the house. He froze, wondering who could possibly be visiting at such an hour, and then he heard another knock and realized that he had better try to seem as relaxed and calm as normal.

Peering into the back room, he saw that Patience was staring at the wall.

"Keep quiet," he said, pulling the door shut before making his way through to the other end of the house. He adjusted his jacket, hoping to make himself look a little better held together, and then he opened the front door to find a familiar figure standing in the yard. "What -"

"I'm going to do it," Arthur Barlow said firmly, clearly highly agitated about something. "I don't care what anyone else says, Horace, but I thought I ought to inform you and your wife first. That house cannot be allowed to stand for even one night longer."

"What are you talking about?" Horace asked. "Do you mean Hadlow House?"

"Peter Finch is worse than dead," Arthur explained, "and the house is to blame. I know it's your property, but if you think about it, with the house gone you can at least sell the land."

"I'm not quite sure that it works like that," Horace said cautiously. "Arthur, I appreciate your concern, but I can't have you running around setting fire to my property. You mustn't listen to all the silly talk about Hadlow House, people tend to get themselves all wound up about nothing and they forget that it's just a pile of bricks sitting out there in the forest."

"I need to talk to Anne."

"My wife? Why?"

"I don't mean to offend you, Horace, but it's my understanding that Anne went to great lengths to retain ownership of that house. She holds the deeds, does she not?"

"She does," he replied cautiously, "but as her husband, I -"

"Then I must speak with her," Arthur continued, stepping forward, only for Horace to put a foot in the way and stop him entering the property. "Horace, I know she feels the same way about that house, she only tolerates its existence because she sees no way to tear it down safely. I am offering to find a way, and to take on any risk that might attach to the endeavor. Can't you see that I'm trying to do the right thing?"

"Anne isn't here."

"When will she be back?"

"She's gone away."

"Away? Where to?"

"To stay with her sister."

"I wasn't aware that Anne had a sister."

"She did, but she's dead."

"Are you sure?"

"She died a long time ago."

"And now Anne has... gone to stay with her?"

"I can't be standing here arguing all afternoon," Horace replied. "I've got a lot of work that needs doing."

"That would be a first for you."

"I beg your pardon?"

"Tell Anne that I must speak to her as soon

as she gets back," Arthur replied. "I'm not sure that I can wait too long, but I'll try. That house is evil, Horace, and something must be done about it. Too many people have chosen to ignore the fact over the years, but I shall not be one of them. Sooner rather than later, I shall have no choice but to go and deal once and for all with that wretched Hadlow House."

***

"He's an idiot," Horace said as he rifled through the desk in his wife's sewing room. "I'm *surrounded* by idiots. The sooner I get out of this miserable little village, the better."

Pushing the first drawer shut, he opened another before turning and looking toward the doorway.

"Charlotte, can you come and help me?" he called out, before stopping and listening to the silence. "Charlotte, you foolish child, where are you? I need you to come here at once!"

Realizing that the girl must be out, he returned his attention to the drawers and continued to search through the various items, tossing aside several objects including a silver ring before finally spotting what he was after. As a growing sense of power began to spread through his body, he held the single page up so that he could see it better; Anne had been absolutely determined to guard the deeds to Hadlow House with her life, seemingly convinced that something awful might happen if they ever fell into the hands of another person. Now, realizing that his entire plan had come to fruition, Horace hesitated for a moment as he felt the enormity of the situation flood through his body.

"It's mine," he whispered with a huge grin. "It's really mine. I can get rid of this miserable life and this miserable village forever, I can really become someone."

He thought for a moment, before straightening his posture to an almost ridiculous degree.

"I can be a true gentleman," he continued, speaking much more clearly now in a poor imitation of how he imagined a London society man might behave. "I can finally be who I was born to be. I can be..."

For a moment, staring down at his own hands, he somehow saw a pile of coins. Thick and golden and almost throbbing with promise, these coins began to spill out of his grasp; he tried to catch them all, quickly dropping to his knees, but already the coins seemed to be melting and slipping through his fingers. Filled with a growing sense of panic, he tried to scoop the glistening liquid back up before resorting to licking the floor in a desperate attempt to drink as much of the gold as possible. Despite a strong metallic taste in his mouth and a growing sense of heaviness in his belly, he persisted for several more seconds before suddenly realizing the foolishness of his actions. Pulling back, he saw that there was no gold and no coins, although when he saw the deeds again he knew that plenty of money would be coming his way soon.

"Gotta keep a good head on my shoulders," he murmured, wiping sweat from his brow as he got to his feet. "There's no sense in pushing ahead of myself."

He adjusted the collar of his shirt, still feeling a little out of sorts, and then he realized that he needed to move swiftly. Anne's body was well-buried and – with a little luck – would never be found again, and Patience was secured until he could be sure that he would no longer need her. Charlotte was an inconvenience, one he briefly considered leaving behind until he could establish himself in London, but he reminded himself that the girl might yet be useful. Besides, he wanted to have someone along for the ride, someone who could witness his transformation, so finally he headed to the door and listened for a moment to the silence of the house.

"Charlotte?" he yelled. "Girl, I need your help! We have to get out of the village for a while, we don't need to take much with us but we have to dig out a few essentials!"

He waited, but the house remained entirely

silent.

"Charlotte?" he shouted, puzzled by her absence, having not even noticed that she'd been gone for most of the day. "What's going on? Where are you?"

CHAPTER NINETEEN

"COWARDS, THE LOT OF them," Arthur Barlow said as he stood in his workshop and held up the largest of his knives, spotting his own reflection in the dull metal. "Let's see how they feel once I've gone out there and destroyed that house."

He paused, feeling a hint of dread in his chest, but he knew that this was no time to back down. In his mind's eye he could still see the horrific injuries that had been suffered by poor Peter Finch; he hadn't dared to return to Cartwright's house to see how the boy was doing, but he told himself that there'd be time for that later. He made an effort to switch the image in his mind, and now he saw Hadlow House burning to the ground, reduced to nothing more than ash, and then he imagined pouring salt onto the ground.

"You'll be gone forever," he said, looking at his own face in the knife's blade again, "and -"

Suddenly seeing a second face in the metal, staring back at him from just over his shoulder, he spun around. There was no sign of anyone else in the workshop, but he felt sure that he'd seen a woman's face. He looked at the knife again, struggling to make anything out now as his hand trembled and the knife shuddered, but after a few seconds he saw his own eyes and he was shocked by a trace of fear in his expression. This fear, he knew, could be his greatest enemy.

"There's no time for any of that," he said, heading to one of the tables and picking up a pot of spirits. These spirits would burn fast and well, he knew from experience, and he needed only to start a fire in the house.

The knife, meanwhile, was supposed to protect him from any evil spirits he might encounter, although deep down he knew that such a weapon would be of limited use.

"In and out quickly," he told himself, as he imagined the flames rising high and consuming the entire structure of Hadlow House. "No messing about or wasting time. In and out in five minutes flat. Less, even. You can do this."

Stepping over to the furnace, he looked at the glowing coals. After a moment, taking a rag, he lit one end and then held it up, watching as the flames ate through the fabric. Holding the rag higher still, until it was above his head, he told himself that he merely needed to remain calm and focused. He looked at the knife again and saw his own eyes, although this time he was surprised to see that the hair was wet and matted on his forehead. He knew he'd been sweating a little, although he couldn't quite understand why he looked so soaked, until finally he noticed a strong smell of spirits filling the air.

Taking a look at the tin, he saw that it was almost empty. A moment ago it had been full; he looked around, wondering what had happened, until he froze as he remembered that – for some reason – he had poured the liquid all over his own head.

"Why did I do that?" he whispered, before spotting the woman's face in the blade again.

Confused, he tried to think back to everything that he'd done over the previous few minutes, and then – in a sudden moment of panic – he looked up at the burning rag in his hand. At that moment the rag fell, landing on his face and igniting the spirits. Letting out a terrified scream, Arthur stumbled back against the wall, but his head and shoulders were already ablaze and he could only drop to his knees as he clawed desperately at the flames and tried to put them out.

Somehow, over the sound of the inferno, he could hear not only his own crackling flesh as it burned, but also a woman's laugh.

***

Still hiding under the table, Charlotte dared not move a muscle as she heard a faint laugh coming from Molly's lips. A few seconds earlier Molly had fallen silent, but now she seemed amused by something and her laughter was only growing and growing.

Looking toward the door, Charlotte began to calculate her quickest route out of the house. She knew she could leave the room in a matter of seconds, but then she was going to have to find a way to open one of the doors. Having tried that before with Peter, she had no idea exactly how to force her way out of the house, yet she knew she couldn't stay with Molly. Whatever was happening, she wanted no part of it, and she told herself that she simply needed to get home to her mother and father, and that then everything would be alright again.

As Molly continued to laugh, evidently preoccupied by some other matter, Charlotte began to crawl to the other end of the table. She was terrified that at any moment she might attract Molly's attention, but after a few more seconds she scrambled out between two empty chairs and crept toward the door, before stopping and looking over her shoulder.

Standing at the table's far end, Molly had her head bowed as she continued to chuckle, almost as if she was lost in some other world.

***

Rolling onto his side as the flames continued to eat through his body, Arthur Barlow reached up and placed his hands on his face. He could no longer see anything, but – as the intensity of the fire began to fade – his burned face emerged from the inferno, blistering all over; desperate to save himself, he started clawing at the wounds in a desperate attempt to scrape off as much of the flammable liquid as possible.

Instead, he was succeeding only in ripping away chunks of flesh.

As the flames continued to die down, Arthur realized once again that he could hear a woman laughing nearby. He turned and tried to look back across the room, but his burned eyes afforded him no such opportunity. Instead he could only listen as the laughter became ever louder, hanging somehow in the air all around. Opening his mouth, he managed to let out one final, low breath before slumping down dead against the floor.

The laughter continued for a few more seconds, before fading to nothing.

***

Taking care to remain as silent as possible, Charlotte began to edge her way along the corridor that led toward the kitchen. She still had no clear idea in her mind, but she told herself that there had to be some way out of the house, even if that meant smashing a window and then breaking the wooden frames.

Reaching the kitchen, she stopped for a moment. She could no longer hear Molly laughing, although she told herself that she was probably just too far away. Instead of allowing herself to worry, she stepped into the kitchen and hurried to the back door, only to find that it was still locked. She looked around, hoping to spot a key, but instead she saw only a few boxes on one of the counters. Picking one of the boxes up, she tested its corners and found that they were firm, and then she turned and saw that the nearby window was her only chance to escape.

Stepping closer, she raised the box and told herself that breaking the window was a small price to pay for getting out of the house. Still, she hesitated for a moment, scared that once the glass shattered she would inevitably drawn attention to herself again.

***

"Arthur, what's going on in there?" Sarah Barlow asked as she made her way through to the workshop. "What's this horrible stench? It's like meat or -"

Stopping in the doorway, she saw her husband's body on the ground. His head was entirely burned, with large blisters on the sides of what had once been his face. For a few seconds Sarah could only stare in horror, until finally she screamed.

***

"I'm going to do it," Charlotte whispered to herself, trying to find enough courage to break the window. "I shan't get into too much trouble, not once I explain."

She hesitated for a few more seconds, before starting to throw the box, only to have it yanked from her hand at the last second. Startled, she spun around and found Molly standing right behind her.

"I'm sorry," Molly murmured, throwing the box to one side, "I just had to take care of something. I must confess, there is great pleasure to be had in puncturing the ego of an overly-confident man."

"Please let me go!" Charlotte sobbed, as all

the pain and fear erupted from her body and tears ran freely down her face. "I didn't want to come here in the first place!"

"Let you go?" Molly replied, seemingly puzzled by this request. "Oh, you poor sweet, dull-minded child." She reached out and put her hands on either side of Charlotte's tear-stained face. "Don't you understand anything at all?" She leaned closer with a large, leering grin. "I was *always* going to let you go! After all, you're not the one I want!"

CHAPTER TWENTY

A GENTLE EVENING BREEZE blew across the garden, carrying thick snow that had been falling all day, as Charlotte's eyes began to flicker open.

Letting out a sudden gasp, she sat up. Having been unconscious on the ground, she was now soaked thanks to the snow, and she immediately began to shiver. She looked around, trying to remember exactly what had happened, but the last thing she remembered was Molly's icy hands on the sides of her face, and then...

And then what?

Looking up, she saw that the sky was turning a darker shade of blue as night began to fall. Having only intended to be away from home for half an hour or so, she realized that she must have been gone for most of the day, which meant that she was going to be in terrible trouble once she returned. Stumbling to her feet, she felt as if her knees might be about to buckle, and as she took a few steps back she realized that she was so incredibly exhausted. Worried that she might collapse again, she looked at the house and saw its wide-open front door, and then she instinctively turned to hurry away and head back to the village.

"Help me!"

Stopping in her tracks, Charlotte immediately recognized that voice. She swallowed hard, and then she turned to see that now Molly was standing alone in the doorway with a terrified expression on her face.

"Charlotte?" Molly continued, shaking so violently that she could barely get any words out at all. "Please..."

Raising her left arm, Molly reached out with one hand.

"Charlotte, I'm so scared," she explained. "You have no idea... I don't know who she is, but this woman has been inside my mind, controlling me and making me do horrible things but... I didn't want to do any of them!"

Charlotte took a step back.

"Don't leave me!" Molly shouted, filled with panic. "Please don't leave me, Charlotte. She was possessing me somehow, and I could only watch and feel as she hurt Peter. She did awful things to his face, and then she threw him from the window. I don't know where he is now, but he must be so scared. She did those things to him using my hands, Charlotte, and I felt all of it. I felt my thumbs bursting his eyes, and I felt my fingers ripping his tongue out, but it wasn't my fault! You have to believe me!"

Charlotte stared at her for a few seconds, before taking another step back.

"Don't go!" Molly called out plaintively. "Charlotte, I'm so scared. I know that if I try to leave, she'll hurt me, but I don't know what she wants! I don't know how to get away!"

As more snow fell between them, the two girls stared at one another in silence.

"I can sense her," Molly continued. "She's right behind me."

Charlotte squinted a little, but she could see only darkness in the doorway behind Molly.

"Please, Charlotte," Molly said, as her voice somehow managed to tremble even harder than before, "you're the only one left here with me now. Please, promise me you won't leave me with this horrible woman."

Charlotte opened her mouth to reply, but she held back for a few seconds.

"I'm so scared," Molly said, before taking a solitary step forward, making her way just beyond the threshold of the house. "Charlotte, are you going to help me? I don't think she's going to leave me alone for very long, I think she was distracted but now she's coming for me all over again. Charlotte, please, I saw what she did to Peter and I'm scared she might do it to me next. Will you help me?"

Before Charlotte had a chance to reply, she spotted a figure stepping up behind Molly. As the woman appeared in the darkened doorway, Charlotte felt a growing sense of dread starting to reach through her chest, and in that moment she knew that she had to get as far away from Hadlow House as possible. Even though deep down she understood that she should help Molly, she was unable to keep from taking a stumbling step back, then another, and then another until she bumped against the wall that encircled the garden.

"Charlotte, please!" Molly sobbed. "Don't leave me!"

"I'm sorry," Charlotte whispered, "I -"

Suddenly the woman pulled Molly back into the house. As she tumbled into the darkness, Molly let out a horrified scream that was immediately cut off as the front door slammed shut. Not even daring to wait and see what happened next, Charlotte turned and raced to the gate, pulling it open and then hurrying out onto the dirt path that led away from Hadlow House. As she ran, snow continued to fall, with some settling high up on the metal sign above the gate.

***

"Help me," Charlotte whimpered a few minutes later, stumbling through the snow as she bumped against trees on either side. "Why won't somebody help me?"

Looking all around, she realized that she had lost the path some time ago, that there was too much snow for her to ever see precisely where she was going. Her feet crunched against the snow that was already on the ground, but more was falling and she worried that soon the entire landscape would be lost in a haze of white. Breathing fast and struggling to hold her thoughts together, Charlotte forced herself to keep going despite the ache in her legs, yet in truth she had lost all sense of direction and she knew that she might even be inadvertently heading straight back toward the terrifying house.

"Won't somebody help me?" she cried, sniffing back more tears. "I just want to go home! I'm only -"

As her foot caught in the snow, she let out a brief gasp as she fell down into the snow. Her clothes were still wet and cold, and as she began to haul herself up she felt as if she was going to be lost forever. She brushed as much snow as possible from her arms, and then she began to push forward again, only to stop suddenly as she spotted a figure standing far ahead between the trees.

Although her first thought was to cry out to this man, something held her back. She felt a dash of fear in her heart, and after a few seconds she saw that the man was missing one arm. She'd seen injured people before, of course, but something about this particular man filled her with a sense of absolute fear, until finally she turned and began to push through the snow again, heading in the opposite direction.

She kept going for the next few minutes, before stopping as she saw the man yet again. He was standing far ahead, and she had no idea how he could have made it around so quickly, but she was once again struck by the absolutely certain belief that she couldn't possibly go anywhere near him. Something about the man seemed to be radiating pure horror, to the extent that Charlotte barely had time to even think before she turned and began to hurry away, pushing through the snow with a growing sense of fear that the man was following close behind.

And then, just as she was starting to lose all hope, she stumbled out onto a stretch of the forest that at first seemed to be just another clearing. She turned and looked both ways, and in an instant she realized that she recognized this as the road that led into the village. She could even just about make out the spire of St. Leonard's in the distance, rising up into the snowy evening sky.

"I made it," she stammered, filled with a sense of huge relief as she realized that somehow she'd managed to find her way out of the forest, even if she'd only done so thanks to her attempts to get away from the strange one-armed man. "I'm home! I'm safe!"

She began to run, unable to hold back as she raced along the road. Even as the ground started to dip beneath her feet, heading down the hill that led into Cobblefield, Charlotte knew that she would only be truly safe once she was back at home with her mother and father. She continually looked over her shoulder, terrified that either Molly or the strange woman from the house might be after her, but finally she reached the little bridge that led toward the village and she had to stop and lean against a wall. For a moment she thought back to the sight of Molly getting dragged back into the house, and then she set off on her way home. She felt sad about Molly, but she was far more concerned about getting home and warming herself by the fire.

The village was dark now, and all she knew was that she had to get back to her parents.

CHAPTER TWENTY-ONE

"WHAT DO YOU MEAN?" Charlotte asked a short while later as she stood in the yard at home, with snow still falling all around. "Where did she go?"

"It's too complicated for you to understand," Horace said, shoving another box onto the back of the cart. "You're just a child."

"But -"

"If you want to bring anything, you need to fetch it now, but there isn't much room."

"But -"

"Get a move on!" he snapped. "I want to get as far away from this hellhole as possible!"

"But..."

Charlotte paused for a moment, trying to make sense of all the information that was flooding through her mind.

"I'm not in trouble?" she asked cautiously.

"Why would you be in trouble?"

"I've been out all day," she told him. "I went to..."

Again she hesitated, before realizing that she should probably be honest.

"I went to the house."

"What house?"

"*That* house."

He turned to her, and for a moment he seemed puzzled.

"Well, you're back now," he said finally, "and that's all that really matters. I hope you learned your lesson, young lady."

"Molly's still -"

"Do you have anything you want to bring?" he continued, cutting her off. "If not, that's fine by me. I'll buy you everything you could ever want once we get to London."

"London?"

Stepping over to her, he crouched down and put his hands on her shoulders, and for a moment his eyes burned bright with the intensity of his greed.

"We're going to be rich, Charlotte," he told her. "Richer than your childish mind can possibly imagine. I can't explain it all now, it's all too complicated and adult, but the point is we're going to be rolling in riches just as soon as I've found Mr.

Wadsworth and given him the deeds. There's a lot of money tied up in that house but soon it's going to be ours! Isn't that the most wonderful feeling ever?"

"I suppose it is," she admitted. "How long are we going to be away for?"

"From this place?" His grin grew. "Forever. Neither of us will ever have to even set foot in this place again, we'll be too busy joining the members of high society in the big city. I'll buy you the finest coat, Charlotte, and you'll be able to court all the rich princes."

"I will?"

"You might even be able to marry yourself one," he continued, as he wiped some dirt from the side of her face. "How does that sound?"

She thought for a moment. Although she wanted to tell him all about Molly and Peter, she was still worried about getting into trouble; besides, the idea of marrying an actual prince was almost too much for her to comprehend, and her head was already filled with the image of herself sitting on a big golden throne with a crown on her head. Courtiers were running around, tending to her every need, and for a few seconds she more or less forgot entirely about the real world; she only stirred from her fantasy when she heard her father swearing as he caught his finger on one of the boxes.

"Charlotte, are you getting ready or not?" he snapped angrily. "We need to hit the road! If there's anything you need to do before we leave, do it now!"

"I have to tell you something," she replied. "I didn't go alone to the house, I went with -"

"I really don't care!" he shouted, before grabbing her by the arm and shoving her across the yard. "You've got five minutes to fetch anything you need, and then we're out of here!"

***

Stepping into the back room, Charlotte froze as soon as she saw Patience tied and bound on one of the chairs. She blinked, watching her great-grandmother and listening as she heard her whispering about something.

"Are you coming with us?" Charlotte asked cautiously, before stepping into the room.

"Oh Daniel," Patience murmured, not even giving any sign that she'd noticed the girl's arrival. "Why aren't you home yet? I've been waiting for so long to see you."

"Who are you talking to?" Charlotte replied.

"How long has it been?" Patience asked. "I'm not so good with time, not these days, but I feel sure that you've been gone for far too long and -"

Suddenly she turned and looked at Charlotte, staring with two milky white eyes. Opening her mouth, Patience seemed to be on the verge of saying something more, but for a few seconds she seemed utterly confused by what was happening.

"Anne?" she said finally. "Is that you?"

"I'm Charlotte," Charlotte said.

"Charlotte?" Patience paused, as if she had never heard that name before in her life, and then she smiled and shook her head. "Of course you are," she continued. "I'm sorry, for a moment there you looked so much like your mother, but most of the time you look far more like your father. What's his name again?"

"Father's name is Horace," she reminded her. "Horace Smudge."

"That's right," Patience replied, breathing a sigh of relief. "And where is your mother?"

She tried to sit up, only for the ropes around her body to hold her down.

"I don't understand," she added, looking down at her own tightly-bound arms. "What's happening to me? Why can't I move properly?"

"Father put you like that, I think," Charlotte told her. "I don't know why, but... do you want me to untie you?"

"I just don't know what this is all about," Patience said. "I'm not even sure how I got here. I think I might have taken a tumble earlier. Did I perchance fall down the stairs?"

"I don't know," Charlotte said, before

hearing footsteps approaching from behind. She turned just as her father joined her in the doorway. "Why is she tied up like that?" she asked. "Did she do something wrong?"

"Not especially," Horace said, watching Patience for a moment before placing a hand on his daughter's shoulder. "I just need her to stay in place for a little while longer, until I'm sure I don't need her. Then I'll come back and... make sure that she's comfortable." He paused, before raising his voice. "Did you hear that, Patience?" he called out. "You don't have to wait much longer, I just need to be absolutely certain that I can sell the house without your help. The last thing I need is to get tripped up at the last moment."

"I don't know what you're talking about," she told him.

"No, of course you don't," he replied.

"Where's Daniel?" she asked, sounding a little more agitated now. "I really must speak to him, I'm sure he'll help me understand everything."

"Who's she talking about?" Charlotte said softly.

"That doesn't matter," Horace replied, watching Patience for a moment before reaching down and taking his daughter by the hand. "Trust me, I've got everything under control. We're going to be rich, and no-one can stop us now. I just need to go to one of the other villages and catch Mr.

Wadsworth before he heads off, and then we'll have enough money to move to London and start our lives all over again."

"And Mother will be there waiting for us, won't she?"

"Of course," he said, before pushing her away from the door. "Go to the cart," he told her. "Be a good girl and don't disobey me."

"Alright," Charlotte said reluctantly as she walked away.

"And Charlotte?" he added.

She turned to him.

"Don't look back," he said firmly. "Just go to the cart and wait there. Is that understood?"

Once his daughter was gone, Horace stepped across the room and looked down at Patience. Still trying to wriggle free from the ropes, Patience glanced around as if she expected to spot someone else, and Horace began to smile once more as he realized that the old woman couldn't possibly break free from her restraints. After watching for a moment longer, he headed to the fireplace and looked at the few logs that were still glowing as the fire continued to dwindle.

"It's cold outside," he murmured, as the flames reflected in his eyes. "I told a little lie just now, Patience. I told the girl that I'd come back to check on you later, but in truth I've realized already that I no longer need you. I have the deeds, so I no longer need anything in this miserable little village." He took a blanket from one of the nearby chairs. "This house is rented," he added, "so I can't sell it. Can you believe that? Anne made us live in a rented house for all these years, when we had a perfectly good house waiting out there in the forest. It was in your family once, but she sold it and then she rented it back because we were short of money." He chuckled. "Isn't that pathetic? We're been scrimping and saving for so many years, when we could have been living lives of luxury all that time."

He paused again, before dipping the blanket into the flames and then moving it away. As the blanket began to burn, he placed it gently on a chair near Patience and watched as the fire spread across the fabric.

"This shouldn't take very long," he said, with smoke already starting to fill the room. "A simple accident, that's how people are going to see your unfortunate demise. It should be quick for you, at least." He turned to her. "Goodbye, Patience," he added. "I'm simply putting you out of your misery. There's no need to thank me. Your death will be thanks enough."

CHAPTER TWENTY-TWO

"SIT TIGHT AND STOP complaining!" Horace snapped angrily as the cart bumped over another rough section of the road leading out of Cobblefield. "Child, you're trying my patience!"

"I'm sorry," Charlotte replied, shivering on the seat next to him. "I'm just cold!"

"Do you think I'm not cold too?" he asked. "With all your whining and whimpering and moaning, have you ever once stopped to ask me how *I'm* doing?"

"No," she replied meekly, as she hugged herself a little tighter and looked into the snowy darkness ahead. "I'm sorry."

"This horse is on the verge of being lame," he muttered. "It should get us to London, but after that it'll only be good for one thing. I suppose I might be able to sell it, if only for a pittance."

Turning to look over her shoulder, Charlotte saw a few lights in the distance. She knew that those lights were in Cobblefield, and that the village she'd called home all her life was now receding fast; she'd listened to her father's constant promises of luxury in London, and she certainly liked that idea, but at the same time part of her was already longing for the familiar streets of the only place she'd ever known. She wished that her mother could be with her to offer a few cheering words, but she told herself that eventually the family would all be reunited in some fancy new house in London.

Looking back at her father, she watched the side of his face and saw an unusual harshness that seemed almost to be spreading out from beneath his skin. A moment later, before she could ask him about her great-grandmother, the cart suddenly lurched to a halt and she saw that her father had tightened the reins.

"What is it?" she asked, before turning to look at the road ahead. "What -"

Before she could finish, she spotted a figure standing by the side of the road. In the darkness, she couldn't make the figure out very well, but something about its shape – even from a distance – reminded her of her own mother.

"It can't be," Horace whispered.

"Father?" Charlotte asked. "What's wrong?"

"Shut up!" he hissed, adjusting his grip on the reins for a moment. "It just can't be. I haven't come this far, just to start seeing ghosts now. I'm a respectable man and I'm simply not going to fall for such foolish superstitions!"

"What are you talking about?"

She looked toward the figure again, and her first thought was that some poor soul was out in the cold. A moment later her father pulled on the reins and the cart started moving, and Charlotte kept her eyes on the figure as they made their way along the road. Although this stranger was standing a little way off, out in the field, as she got closer Charlotte felt more and more certain that she was looking at her own mother.

"Wait!" she said, touching her father's arm. "Isn't that -"

"No!" he snapped.

"It looks like Mother!"

"Don't be so stupid," he replied. "What would your mother be doing standing in some random field in the snow?"

As the cart continued on its way, Charlotte had to turn and crane her neck in order to still see the figure. Now that they were moving away, she was less able to make out the figure's features, yet the sense of familiarity lingered and she still felt that she was looking at her mother. At the same time, she knew that there was no good reason why her mother would be standing in a field in the snow, and a few seconds later the image was entirely swallowed up by the darkness of the night.

Turning to her father again, Charlotte told herself that she had to trust him. After all, if that *had* been her mother, why would her father simply keep driving the cart away along the road?

"I don't want to hear any more of your complaining," Horace said firmly. "You're a very lucky young lady, Charlotte. It's about time you showed some gratitude!"

***

"Daniel?" Patience said, still pulling on the ropes that kept her bound against the chair. "My darling, where are you?"

As flames continued to roar on the other side of the room and the heat began to build, Patience found herself sweating. She still wasn't entirely sure what was happening, yet deep down some instinctive sense of fear was starting to stir, as if some primordial part of her soul recognized the danger posed by the fire. She looked around, still hoping against hope that her husband might arrive and make everything alright, and then – filled with the sudden sense that she had to get out of the room – she leaned forward and managed to pull herself from the chair, until she toppled forward and landed with a heavy thump against the wooden floorboards.

"Daniel!" she shouted, just about managing to sit up now. "Anne, where are you? Is anybody there? Please, I... I don't quite know what to do!"

She stared at the flames for a moment longer, horrified by the sight of them eating their way through the furniture. The heat against her face was starting to feel rather uncomfortable, and she was beginning to feel a strange separation between the two parts of her body: her conscious thoughts were still mired in confusion, but her flesh – the bones and meat and blood of her body – was filled with a desperate need to escape. And then, as Patience found herself wondering exactly how she might get away from the heat, she felt the ropes slip free from around her wrists.

"What -"

Holding her hands up, she saw that they were now entirely free. She began to get to her feet, and sure enough the rest of the ropes fell away, as if they had been loosened by some hidden hand. Now the heat was stronger still, and after a moment Patience had no choice but to turn and stumble out of the room, quickly heading along the corridor and into the kitchen, where she stopped to try to gather her thoughts.

Even now, she could hear the roaring and crackling of the flames.

"Daniel?" she said, as tears began to run

down her cheeks. "Where are you? What -"

Before she could finish, she suddenly remembered: in her mind's eye she saw Daniel dead on the ground, having been laid out on the grass outside Hadlow House. This vision was so shocking and so horrifying that she immediately tried to thin of something else, yet somehow the truth was breaking through and finally she understood that Daniel wasn't coming back at all. He was dead, and she felt a creeping sense of terror as she realized that something seemed almost to be reaching out to her from several miles away, almost as if...

"You," she whispered as she remembered the sight of Fanny Baxter standing at the window of that awful house. "You're still there, aren't you? You're still haunting that place, even after all these years."

She swallowed hard, but the fog had lifted in her mind and she was filled now with a sense of determination. She had no idea exactly how many years she had spent wasting away in the little house in Cobblefield, but when she looked down at her own hands she saw that they were the hands of an old woman. She vaguely remembered having noticed this before, but now she felt driven by the need to deal with the horror of Hadlow House once and for all. She also knew, deep down, that she had to act while her mind was clear, for she worried that at any moment she might slip back into her awful near-fugue state.

"It would seem," she said after a moment, thinking once more of Fanny out at the house, "that you leave me with little choice."

She thought back to the way the ropes had fallen away from her body, and she understood that in all likelihood Fanny had reached out to free her. If that was the case, was it not likely that Fanny *wanted* her to go to the house? No matter, she quickly decided; she had tried leaving Hadlow House alone and abandoned, but now for the first time she understood that the ghost of Fanny Baxter would never be satisfied. Instead, that awful specter needed to be confronted and destroyed.

Turning, she saw a faint orange glow in the corridor. She knew that somebody needed to put out the fire, but she also knew that Anne and Horace and Charlotte were long gone. Exactly where they had gone, she could not be sure, yet she at least understood that they were safe from the flames. And with that thought in her mind, she began to shuffle toward the front door, bracing herself for the long and slow walk out to that awful house in the forest.

CHAPTER TWENTY-THREE

"WHERE IS MR. WADSWORTH?" Horace shouted, banging on the door of the public house in the neighboring village of Boreham. "Wake up immediately, I must speak with him! Where is the fellow?"

Hearing the sound of a window opening, he stepped back and looked up just in time to see a man leaning out from the building.

"What are you doing out there?" the man snapped. "Can't you see that we're closed?"

"Indeed," Horace replied, "but this is a most urgent matter."

"So urgent that you're out in such awful weather?" The man looked over at the cart and saw Charlotte shivering in the snow. "So urgent that you'd subject a child to -"

"I don't care about any of that!" Horace snarled angrily. "I'm sorry to have woken you, but I must catch up to Mr. Wadsworth as quickly as possible. I have something for him, something that he has wanted for quite some time, and it's absolutely imperative that I speak to him. Please, he told me that he would be staying here for a while."

"A Mr. Wadsworth departed this afternoon," the man explained wearily. "He said he was going back to London and that -"

"Then I must catch him!" Horace yelled, turning and racing back to the cart and immediately climbing up onto his seat. "That idiot has already departed," he told Charlotte as he fumbled for the reins, "but we can still catch him if we are quick"

"I'm tired," she replied.

"I don't care!"

"Father, I think I saw Mother back there," she continued. "In the field."

"Are you going on about this again?" he asked, turning and glaring at her. "I had no idea that my only child had grown up to be such a fool!"

"I'm also worried about Molly."

"Who?"

"My friend," Charlotte reminded him. "I think... I think she's at the house. At Hadlow House, I mean. I didn't have a chance to tell you earlier, because we were in too much of a hurry, but I think someone should go and make sure that she's alright.

And Peter, too. Something really strange happened at that house and I don't want Molly or Peter to be hurt!"

Horace sighed.

"And what about everyone else?" she continued. "Great-grandmother Patience should be with us!"

"Alright," Horace replied, putting a hand on her shoulder, "let us be clear on this matter. You're old enough to make your own decision now, Charlotte, but you must make it quickly. Either you can climb down and walk back to Cobblefield, and try to help Molly and Peter and Patience and anyone else you want to waste your time on, and you can go and look for your mother's ghost in some field... or you can come with me to London, and we'll have riches beyond our wildest dreams, and you won't ever have to think about those poor wretches we'll be leaving behind tonight. You can make up your own mind, Charlotte, but you must do it now! What do you want? Friends or money?"

She opened her mouth to reply, but at the last second she thought of herself struggling through the snow on her way back to Cobblefield. She knew the walk would take several hours, and she was so very cold and tired, and the thought of having lots of money in London was certainly very appealing. She knew that her mother would turn back if she happened to be in the same situation, but in that moment Charlotte realized that she could just stop worrying and – instead – take the easy option.

"What time shall we reach London?" she asked cautiously.

"That's my girl," he replied, tousling the hair on top of her head for a moment before pulling on the reins, spurring the horse to start pulling the cart along again. "You take after me a lot more than you take after your mother's side of the family, Charlotte, and that's a good thing. As for London, we shall be there as soon as we have spoken to Mr. Wadsworth. And by the time the sun comes up tomorrow morning, we'll be rich!"

***

As she stumbled along the narrow streets of Cobblefield, Patience pulled her shawl tight in an attempt to protect herself from the cold. She so desperately wanted to go and find somewhere warm, but she knew that Hadlow House was out there in the night waiting for her return, and she told herself that she had to get there before her mind became muddled again.

"Fire!" a voice shouted in one of the other streets. "There's a fire at the stable-yard!"

"Fetch water!" another voice yelled.

"Get to the well!" a third voice called out. "Hurry, there might be people trapped inside! The fire has already spread to the roof!"

As figures raced through the darkness, Patience turned and opened her mouth to call out to them. She wanted to let them know that nobody was trapped inside the building, that she had been the last, but the figures were already gone. She could hear more voices calling to one another, and after a moment she realized that she could see the glow of a considerable blaze starting to rise up into the snow-filled night sky. She thought of that beautiful house going up in flames, but she knew that at her advanced age there was nothing she could do to help; all she could manage was to get out to Hadlow House and deal with the ghost of Fanny Baxter once and for all.

She turned to keep walking, before spotting a familiar figure hurrying along the street.

"Patience Purkiss, is that you?" Muriel Ward said, stopping and placing a hand on her arm. "What are you doing out at this late hour? I heard there's a fire somewhere in the village!"

"Indeed there is," Patience told her.

"Are you alright?" Muriel continued, clearly concerned for the older woman's well-being. "You must be absolutely freezing."

"Oh, I shall be fine," Patience said, not wanting to cause any concern. "You mustn't worry about me."

"I don't know what's going on in this village

today," Muriel sighed. "First there was that horrid business with poor Peter Finch, then little Molly Mason disappeared, then Arthur Barlow was found dead and now there's a fire."

"What happened to Peter Finch?" Patience asked.

"I don't think anyone truly knows just yet," Muriel replied. "Some say that it's to do with..."

Her voice trailed off for a moment as she realized that she might be about to stumble into a rather sensitive conversation.

"I understand," Patience told her as more snow drifted down all around them. "And what of poor Arthur Barlow."

"He -"

"No," Patience added suddenly, cutting her off as more and more voices joined the chorus in the distance, shouting for water and assistance, "actually, I rather think that I can already guess roughly what has happened. I can only promise that after tonight, this village will be free forever from the influence of that malign house."

"What do you mean?" Muriel asked.

"I am only sorry," Patience replied, "that I did not act sooner. Please, I hope that you and the others can forgive me for my cowardice, but I am going to put things right now."

"Muriel!" a voice called out from the corner. "Hurry, you're needed!"

"You must go," Patience told her, "and please, do not worry about me. I am absolutely fine."

"Make sure you get somewhere warm," Muriel replied, hurrying past her and quickly making her way along the street, rushing toward the spot where some men were trying to bring water up from the village's only well. "I shall call on you tomorrow morning, Patience! Just to check that you're in good spirits!"

"That is most kind of you," Patience whispered under her breath, "although I rather doubt that you will need to do anything of the sort."

She hesitated for a moment, listening to the cries in the distance, and then she shuffled along the street. Every bone in her body was screaming at her to turn around, but she forced herself to keep going until she stopped once more to rest, this time in front of the church. Looking up at the spire, she thought of all the times she had gone into that church and asked for guidance, and she thought too of her parents' graves in the cemetery. Although her aged body was so very tired, she knew that she had a duty to finally deal with the danger of Hadlow House once and for all.

"Lord," she whispered, "grant me the strength to do what is right, no matter the temptation otherwise."

She waited for an answer, but all she heard

were more panicked shouts over on the far side of the village. And then, still worried that her mind might at any moment sink back into confusion, she set off along the road that led out toward the forest. As she walked across the bridge, she glanced down and saw the frozen moonlit river below.

CHAPTER TWENTY-FOUR

"FATHER, AREN'T WE GOING too fast?" Charlotte asked, clinging to the cart's railing as the wheels once again bucked over a rough patch on the moonlit road. "Father, I'm scared!"

"No daughter of mine is going to admit to such a thing," Horace told her. "Besides, I'm worried that Mr. Wadsworth will be traveling as quickly as possible on his journey back to London. We need to catch up to him before he gets there."

"But why?" Charlotte asked as the cold wind whipped against her face and the moonlight faded for a moment. "I don't understand. Can't you just talk to him in London?"

"Once he's in London, he can talk to other men and devise a strategy to cheat me," he said firmly. "That's all those people ever want to do, they look at a man like me – a good, simple, honest man – and they think they can rip me off. They'll be coming up with all sorts of ways to offer me barely half of what that house is worth, and they might even succeed if they gang up on me. But if I manage to get to Mr. Wadsworth on my own, and if I'm able to talk to him properly, then I can guarantee every penny that's coming to me!"

"Yes, but -"

Before she could finish, Charlotte was almost jolted straight out of her seat and off the side of the cart. She clung harder to the railing as she tried once more to steady herself.

"They look down on men like me," Horace continued, watching the icy road ahead. "They sneer and hold their noises, and they act as if a man born in a small village can't ever rise to join them in their fancy London halls. Well, that might have been true once, but I swear that one day I'll be dining with the king himself!" He glanced over at his daughter and laughed. "Do you hear that?" he asked. "I'll be sitting next to the king at a fancy banquet, and if you play your cards right I might even be able to get you invited along as well! Would you like that, Charlotte?"

"Yes," she stammered, although in truth she only said this because she knew it was what he wanted to hear. At that moment, all she really cared about was reaching their destination and getting off the cart, and she felt her stomach twitch a little as if she might be on the verge of throwing up.

The road ahead was dark, with the moon once again hidden behind thick clouds.

"You're gonna be a pretty girl when you're older, you know," Horace said, glancing at her briefly before looking ahead again. "Real pretty. In fact, I wouldn't be surprised if you start turning heads. We can use that to our advantage. Would you be up for trying to get all the way to the top in society? I think I know a few tricks. There'll be men who won't mind paying a little extra money for some of your very valuable time."

"I don't mind," she replied, although in truth she failed to really understand what he meant.

"Life's going to be good for us, Charlotte," Horace continued, as he once again adjusted his grip on the reins. "You know, one day we won't even remember that Cobblefield exists. Do you like that idea? We'll have moved so far up the social ladder that all we'll remember will be London." He turned and grinned at her. "We'll be -"

"Look out!" she gasped, suddenly seeing that the road ahead curved dramatically to the right.

"Damn it!" Horace shouted, pulling on the reins as the horse turned to follow the route. "It's so dark, I don't -"

In that instant, the entire cart broke free on one side and flipped, tipping over and throwing both Horace and Charlotte off the side of the road. Screaming, Charlotte felt for a moment as if she was flying through an empty void, before finally she smashed down onto the surface of a frozen river with such force that she instantly felt the ice crack beneath her. She tried to get up, but she felt a sharp pain in her left leg as she began to slip, and a fraction of a second later the rest of the cart smashed down on top of her, shattering the ice and forcing her down beneath the surface.

As soon as she was submerged in the freezing water, Charlotte felt as if every inch of her body had stiffened in shock. The cart was sinking on top of her, pushing her ever downward until she bumped against the riverbed and hit some rocks. Hearing a tremendous roaring sound, she looked up just in time to see the vast shape of the cart slowly cartwheeling through the water above her, silhouetted against the underside of the now-moonlit ice. Debris was floating through the water, and for a moment Charlotte could only stare in horror at the eerily beautiful scene.

A moment later she felt dirty, icy water gushing into her mouth. Filled with panic, she kicked against the riverbed and tried to swim back up, only to feel something clamp tight around her ankle. Startled, she turned and looked down, and to her horror she saw her father holding onto her as he reached out from beneath the cart. As soon as

Horace tried to scream, a rush of bubbles burst from his mouth; Charlotte could just about hear his gurgled cry, but as she tried to pull away from his hand she found that his grip was far too tight.

Pulled back down until she bumped against the riverbed, she knew that she was already running out of breath. She turned and saw her father again, just about able to pick his face out in the faint glow of moonlight that reached through the ice and penetrated the river's depths.

Horace tried again to scream, twisting first one way and then the other as he tried in vain to pull himself out from beneath the sunken cart. Still keeping a tight grip on his daughter's leg, he tried to use her to drag his wrecked body free, and after a moment he reached out with his other hand and grabbed her hand.

Desperately running out of breath now, she instinctively pulled away and then tried to kick her father aside. She knew that she was on the verge of drowning, and she felt filled by a frantic sense of self-preservation. She kicked her father again and again, finally slamming her heel against his face, and after a moment she felt his fingers loosen around her ankle; with one last kick she managed to break free, and she heard his gurgling scream as she turned and kicked the riverbed, launching herself up in a cloud of disturbed sediment.

She could see the surface getting closer and

closer. Determined to swim up as fast as possible, frantic to get air back into her lungs, she kicked her legs as hard as she could manage. The surface seemed as if it should be within touching distance now, yet still she rose through the moonlit water as she felt her lungs almost bursting. Reaching out, she tried to feel the surface, only to suddenly bump hard against the underside of the ice.

Panicking, she tried to find the hole she'd fallen through. She knew it must be close, but as she held her hand out in every direction she felt only more and more ice. She began to swim, bumping against the bottom of the ice, convinced that at any moment she was going to find a gap and swim up to safety. Evidently the gap had been large enough to let an entire cart through, so she supposed that it must be easy to find, yet somehow the ice seemed to spread out far and wide in every direction. Looking up, she saw some cracks, but these were far too thin and she couldn't work out where they came from.

Finally, as she began to gulp icy water into her lungs, she reached up and banged her fists against the ice in one last attempt to break through. She knew that plenty of air was on the other side, just inches away, yet she felt a growing sense of sheer terror as her fists slammed helplessly against the icy barrier. She was losing the last of her strength now, and she was unable to stop herself swallowing more water, but she knew that she'd be alright if she could just break through the ice.

Letting out one last scream, she started clawing at the ice, hoping to dig her way through even as she felt a vast pain starting to burst through her lungs. As she scraped frantically at the ice, she knew she was making no progress at all, yet she couldn't stop herself as she tried desperately to find some way out from beneath the river's frozen surface.

CHAPTER TWENTY-FIVE

SNOW CONTINUED TO FALL, mixing with patches of moonlight as Patience Purkiss shuffled slowly out into the clearing. Stopping, she felt a deadly shudder pass through her chest as she saw the wall ahead, and the gate, and the familiar shape of Hadlow House looming further off in the darkness.

"Here I am again," she said, speaking to herself in a desperate attempt to keep her mind focused and clear. "Did I truly once believe that I could avoid this moment?"

She thought of all the years she had spent living her life in Cobblefield, and she knew now that she had been hiding. What other word could there possibly be? Although she had told herself that

217

she was merely avoiding the house, and that by keeping others away she was managing the situation, deep down she understood now that she had only been delaying the inevitable moment of her return. Somehow Hadlow House had always been waiting for her out in the darkness, occasionally picking off a few other stray souls but only as a means of keeping itself fed until her own return. And now, finally, she was back.

For a moment, she thought back to her terrified climb up through the chimney on that awful night when she'd first escaped from the house. She'd reached the roof, and then she'd seen Daniel waiting for her down in the garden.

"Patience!" Daniel shouted from below, having spotted her. "Down here!"

"I'm going to have to jump," she called out to him, stepping carefully toward the edge. "I don't think -"

She'd jumped, and he'd just about caught her, and in that moment – in his arms – she'd finally felt safe.

"Nice night for a landing," he stammered.

"Are you trying to impress me?" she asked, stunned that she had finally managed to get out of Hadlow House. She hesitated for a moment, and then she sighed. "Because if you are," she

continued, "then I have to tell you, I think it might be working."

For a moment, past and present began to merge in her thoughts.

"Daniel," she whispered now, remembering the sensation of his touch and allowing it to wash over her for a few seconds before finding herself once again standing in front of the gate. A shudder passed through her body, and as she looked at the pitch-black facade of Hadlow House she felt absolutely certain that Fanny Baxter's ghost was still in there, still waiting for her, perhaps even watching her now from one of the windows. She once again considered turning and walking away, but deep down she knew that after almost eighty years she had to finally go back into the house and confront the ghost she'd been running from.

Eighty years.

How had eighty years gone by?

As she opened the gate, she heard its rusty hinges creak loudly in the cold night air. Snow was still falling as she stepped through into the overgrown garden, and she had to force herself to keep going as she picked her way along the old path that led toward the front door. Every step brought a fresh feeling of dread, but finally she stopped and looked up at the closed door, and she thought of

Fanny waiting there. Before even trying the door, however, she made her way around to the side of the house and stopped at one of the windows, and she thought back to the very first night when she'd been on the other side of the glass and had seen Daniel staring in at her.

For a fraction of a second she thought she saw his young, keen face reflected in one of the panes. The glass had become a little distorted over the years, looking almost like ice now. She smiled at the idea of seeing Daniel again, but she quickly reminded herself that this was a memory, not a ghost, and that she had to remember the difference.

"You're here, aren't you?" she said, looking at the window and seeing nothing on the other side. "I can sense you, Fanny Baxter. You're right here, inches away, staring out at me. Why don't you show your miserable face?"

She waited, convinced that at any moment Fanny's glaring features would lean forward toward the window, revealing her awful face in the moonlight. When that failed to happen, however, she simply turned and pushed her way back through the snow, heading around to the front of the house. She already knew what she was going to find; sure enough, as she stopped at the step once more, she saw that the front door was now wide open, revealing the house's darkened interior.

"I know, I know," she said, trying to find the last scrap of strength that she needed. "It's time."

***

A floorboard at the foot of the staircase creaked loudly beneath Patience's right foot.

"Oh," she said, stopping and looking down. She moved her foot a couple more times, creating the creaking sound again. "I remember you. Father was going to fix you, wasn't he? But he never got around to it."

She made the sound a few more times.

"You were so scary in the middle of the night," she told the floorboard, as she managed a brief smile. "Imagine that. A simple loose piece of wood that terrified the life out of me." She began to laugh as she remembered her younger self standing in the exact same spot. "Well, Mr. Floorboard," she continued, "I think -"

Suddenly she heard a bumping sound coming from somewhere to her right. Turning, she looked through an open doorway and realized that the sound had come from the old study. She stepped over to take a closer look – before she had time to back out – and she found herself peering into the room and seeing what appeared to be a pile of boxes over in the corner. Puzzled, she made her way across the room and took a closer look, and as she touched the boxes and felt their dampness she found herself remembering something she'd heard many years ago.

"They've got explosives," someone had explained, back when those two American men had taken refuge in the house. "They mean to blow up King George."

"You didn't get very far with that plan, did you?" she muttered, as she remembered the two men hanging from the posts in front of *The Shoemaker*. "Wretched villains, although your brothers in arms certainly achieved their goal. We shall see how the colonies get on, although in a strange way I certainly understand their desire to break free and control their own -"

Hearing another bump, she turned and looked back out toward the hallway.

"Is that you?" she whispered, although she still saw no sign of Fanny. She waited, and now she heard nothing. "Is that you?" she called out, raising her voice. "Why play games? I'm here, I came back, just the way you always wanted. Do you mean to make me look a fool, and leave me wandering from room to room in search of you?"

She paused, before leaving the boxes and heading back out into the hallway, where she stopped to look up the stairs.

"Is this some game?" she asked. "Am I supposed to hunt for you? I'm far too old for that, Mrs. Baxter. You might have noticed the many lines on my face. It's a miracle that I'm still alive at all, though I wonder now whether I have been clinging on in anticipation of this moment." She took a step forward, causing the board at the bottom of the stairs to creak yet again. "I always thought it was you who waited for me," she continued. "Now, however, I find myself wondering whether it might have been the other way around. Or have we merely been locked together?"

Stopping and looking toward the kitchen, she felt a growing sense of frustration as she realized that evidently Fanny was determined not to show herself.

Not yet, at least.

"My mind is not as it was," she explained. "It is as if there is weather in my thoughts, clouding my memories most often. Snow, perhaps. Yes, that is a good way of explaining it. There is a kind of whiteness that fills my head and robs me of much of myself. I am experiencing a moment of clarity right now, but I cannot guarantee that this will last. If you want me, and if you want me to really know what you are doing, to really understand your revenge... I would advise you to get on with things."

Again she waited, and she could tell that she was being watched. After just a few seconds this sensation began to focus itself a little more, and as she looked at the entrance to the kitchen she felt sure that two eyes were staring back at her. She opened her mouth to call out, but at the same time part of her hated the idea of seeming weak in front of Fanny. Finally, determined to show a little more strength, she stepped forward and waited to see that awful ghostly form again after so many years.

"I must be older than you were when you died," she pointed out. "I think -"

Suddenly she stopped as she saw the faintest outline of a figure. Puzzled, she watched as this figure shuffled forward, and in that moment she realized that this was not Fanny Baxter at all.

"Please," Molly Mason sobbed, as tears rolled down her face. "She... I... You have to help me!"

CHAPTER TWENTY-SIX

"WHAT ARE YOU DOING here?" Patience asked, hurrying forward and putting a hand on the girl's shoulder, finding her to be extremely cold. "This is no place for a child."

"Please," Molly replied, staring up at her with a terrified expression, "I want to go home but she won't let me."

"I met someone tonight," Patience said, already finding that her memories were becoming a little foggy again. She concentrated, and after a few seconds she recalled a woman in the village. "Muriel," she whispered. "Jasper Ward's girl. She told me about... Molly, you're the daughter of Thomas Mason and his wife, are you not?"

Taking a deep breath, she found focusing on family relationships between people helped her to remember exactly who she was dealing with.

"That's right," she continued, pulling the girl closer. "I'm terribly sorry, you'll have to bear with me a little while I try to make sense of things. I believe Muriel even mentioned that you were missing, and she said something about the Finch boy as well."

"I came out here with Peter Finch and Charlotte Smudge," Molly sobbed, putting her arms around Patience and hugging her tight. "I don't know where they are now. I think... I think Peter was thrown out of the window and Charlotte ran away."

"Charlotte?" Patience swallowed hard. "Why would that foolish girl ever have come here in the first place? Her problem is that she has always taken as much after her father as her mother, and it's that side of her that will always lead her into trouble. Are you sure that they're both gone?"

"I'm sure," Molly whimpered, "but the horrible woman won't let me leave. She was controlling me for a while and making me do horrible things, and now she just makes me stay here. Every time I try to go to one of the doors, she appears and shouts at me."

"Is that right?" Patience asked, looking around once more and watching for any sign of Fanny's presence. She knew she had spoken to

Charlotte earlier, back at the house, but her sense of time was still a little twisted. "That sounds about right. Terrorizing innocent people was always her way of doing things, but you mustn't fret too much. We're going to get you out of here."

"I just want to go home," Molly sobbed. "I wish I'd never come to this horrible house in the first place."

"Come on," Patience said, taking the girl's hand and starting to lead her back across the hallway, toward the open front door at the far end. "I rather feel that now I'm here, you'll be surplus to _"

Suddenly the front door slammed shut with terrifying force, rattling its frame in the process. Startled, Patience stopped and immediately felt Molly's hand gripping her tighter than ever. A moment later, before she had a chance to react properly, she heard a roaring sound coming from one of the other rooms and she turned just in time to see a flickering orange glow in a nearby doorway.

"And what's that about?" she muttered under her breath, as she realized that Fanny was most definitely up to something. "It's alright, Molly, I'm still going to get you out of here. I think I'm just going to have to... understand things a little better first." She turned to the girl. "Stay with me," she added, "and you'll be safe. You trust me, don't you?"

"I suppose so," Molly said cautiously,

although she didn't seem entirely convinced.

Still holding the girl's hand, Patience began to make her way across the hallway. Reaching one of the open doors, she looked through into the reception room and saw that somehow – impossibly – a fire was burning in the hearth. She glanced around the room and saw the same old furniture that she remembered from years ago, including the very chair in which her father had sat once while talking to the priest. She tried to remember the priest's name, but this proved elusive, although she recalled that he had met a rather unfortunate fate.

"It's warm!" Molly gasped, pulling her hand free and rushing forward, then dropping to her knees and starting to heat her hands in the glow of the fire. "This is the first time I've been warm since I got here!"

"Be careful," Patience said.

"I'm so cold," Molly continued, leaning even closer to the fire, until her hands were almost in the flames. "I know it's snowing outside, but in here it's colder than anywhere I've ever been before."

"Be careful," Patience said again, before making her way over and pulling the girl back a little. "Sometimes things in this house can be... a little different to how you imagine."

"What do you mean?"

Taking hold of Molly's hands, Patience

turned them around to reveal that the tips of the girl's fingers had begun to blister a little.

"They hurt!" Molly gasped, suddenly pulling away.

"You might very well have burned them off entirely," Patience said, watching the flames for a moment, "and she wouldn't have let you realize until your wrists were down to the bone. That's how she plays her little games. I don't know how she does it, exactly, but she can get into your head."

"I want to go home!" Molly sobbed, getting to her feet and stepping toward the door. "Please, I just -"

Suddenly letting out a gasp, she stumbled back against the wall.

"Is the hole upstairs fixed?" Patience mused, looking up toward the ceiling. For a moment she thought of the gap in the bedroom wall, the same gap through which she'd felt Fanny's hand grab her ankle. "If not, smoke from this fire will be filling that room."

"There's someone out there!" Molly whimpered. "I saw her!"

Turning, Patience looked out into the hallway. She saw no sign of anyone; she could make out the boxes in the study, in the opposite room, but there was no dark figure standing in the way. Still, she had no doubt whatsoever that Fanny was aware of her presence, and after a few seconds she realized that she could almost feel Fanny's eyes staring into her soul.

"Let the girl go," she said firmly, hoping that Fanny could hear and that she might relent. "You don't really care about her, do you? Let's be honest, I'm the only one you want."

"Are you talking to her?" Molly cried. "Can you make her let me go?"

"Perhaps," Patience replied, before stepping over to the door and looking out into the hallway. "Or perhaps she's keeping you here for a reason. I rather fear that there is a purpose behind every action that Fanny Baxter takes, even if that purpose might not be clear to the rest of us."

"I wish I'd never come here today," Molly said, crawling a little closer to the fire and warming her hands again, but this time staying a little further back. "I could be at home right now, with my parents. They're going to be so angry at me when I finally return to them. Can you tell them that I was trapped here all along, and that none of this was my fault?"

"I'm sure they'll understand that," Patience said, still watching for any sign of Fanny's presence.

"It was really all Charlotte's fault," Molly continued. "And Peter too. They both made me come out here when all I wanted to do was stay at home."

"Where are you?" Patience whispered under

her breath, still wondering why Fanny was so far remaining in the shadows. "I'm here, this is all you wanted, so why are you suddenly being so shy? Is it -"

Before she could finish, she heard the faintest bumping sound coming from somewhere upstairs. She looked up toward the top of the staircase, and in that moment she felt a shudder run through her chest as she saw two feet dangling down. In that moment, she understood that this was the ghost of her mother, who had hung herself in that spot so many years ago. For a few seconds she felt compelled to rush up to the landing, to try to find some way to help; she knew that her mother was long dead, of course, yet she still worried for her soul. At the same time, however, she also understood that this vision was most likely being engineered by Fanny. Sure enough, a moment later the feet disappeared and Patience was left standing in the doorway.

"I'm sorry, Mother," she said softly. "I hope you're not trapped here for all eternity in the company of that... ghoul..."

She paused, before realizing that Molly had fallen silent. She turned to reassure the girl again, only to find her standing directly behind her, staring up at her with an unusually calm expression. The change in Molly's demeanor was striking, and after just a couple of seconds Patience began to wonder whether she somehow recognized the look in the girl's eyes.

"That's impossible," she stammered.

"Hello, Patience," Molly replied, her voice suddenly sounding harsh and scratched, as if it was coming from some deeper, darker place. "I'm so glad that you could finally come back to me after all these years."

CHAPTER TWENTY-SEVEN

"LEAVE HER ALONE!" PATIENCE said firmly, as she realized that Fanny's spirit had somehow taken possession of Molly's body. "You don't have to do this! You can torment me all you want without living through this poor young child!"

"I can do a lot of things," Molly replied, "but you have to let me amuse myself somehow. After all, I've been left alone for so very long."

"What -"

"Little Peter had an unfortunate accident," she continued, holding up her hands to reveal the tips of her fingers. "I didn't actually take anything from him, however. He left with everything he had when he arrived, although some of it he had to... carry in a different manner."

"Where's Charlotte?" Patience asked.

"Where's my great-granddaughter?"

"I let her go as a sign of good faith," Molly sneered. "Didn't you speak to her already since then? I sent her back to you, as a message, but..."

Her voice trailed off for a few seconds.

"So cold," she added, before a smile began to grow across her face. "Oh dear, that didn't quite go as I expected. The girl wasn't like you, Patience, was she? She wasn't pure of heart. I'm terribly sorry, but I don't think things have worked out too well for her or her father. None of that is my doing, though. You must believe that. They seem to have met an unfortunate end without any involvement from me at all."

"What are you talking about?" Patience asked.

"None of that matters now," Molly replied, before reaching out and taking Patience's hand. "You are the owner of this house, and as the housekeeper I am duty-bound to take care of you. Don't you understand that all I've ever wanted is to perform my duties?"

"You killed my father!"

"I looked after your father. I cared for him."

"And tortured him!"

"He tortured himself," she explained. "He could have accepted my assistance, yet instead he chose to push me away. I must admit that I was very much offended by that, and in the end I let him go as well. Another gesture of goodwill on my part, even if generally I have not been recognized for my generosity."

"You took him away from me!" Patience snarled. "I didn't see my father for more than half a century, by the time he came back he was nothing more than skin and bones!"

"As -"

"And you took my mother too!" Patience added, stepping toward her. "Did you think that letting me see her again tonight would somehow make things better? I remember how you ruined her life, how you burned her and left her with nothing to live for! My father brought us all here to start new lives, and we would have been perfectly happy if you hadn't been haunting the house, if you hadn't seen fit to interfere!"

"Patience -"

"I know exactly what you are!" she snapped, reaching out and putting both hands on Molly's throat, struggling to hold back the urge to squeeze tighter and tighter. "I don't care how you died, or when, or why, but you had no right to meddle with my family like that!"

"I am the housekeeper and -"

"You're a monster!" Patience shouted, summoning the last of her strength as she pushed Molly back against the wall and began to grip her throat even harder. "How many more people have you hurt over the years, Fanny? How many more lives have you ruined? How long have you spent haunting this house?"

"Please -"

"And how long do you intend to go on haunting it?" Patience asked, squeezing tighter until she felt herself starting to crush the girl's throat. "I'm an old woman, so who's next? I have no bloodline of my own, my father took care of that when he drove a knife into my belly, so who will you torture after I'm gone? Will you just wait around for someone else to come and fall into the trap of this house? Will you lure somebody here so that you can become *their* housekeeper? Or will you simply fade away like the ghost that you are?"

"Stop!" Molly gasped.

"Tell me!" Patience shouted as she felt the girl desperately struggling to push her back.

"Let go of me!" Molly gurgled. "I just want to go home!"

"You have no -"

Stopping suddenly, Patience realized what she was doing; as soon as she let go of Molly's throat, the girl slithered down onto the floor and tried frantically to get her breath back. Patience looked at her own aged, trembling hands and understood in that moment that once again she had fallen into one of Fanny's traps. Just as – many years ago – her father had been driven to stab her, now she herself had very nearly throttled an innocent child to death. She looked at Molly again and saw that she was still struggling, and she also saw red marks around her neck.

"I'm sorry," Patience said, horrified by what she'd so nearly done. "I'm so *very* sorry."

"Please don't hurt me!" Molly sobbed.

"I'm not going to hurt you," Patience replied. "I promise, I would never do that." She reached toward Molly, only to stop as the girl flinched and pulled away. "Please don't be frightened of me," she continued, "I meant you no harm at all, I was only trying to help you but... she tricked me and..."

For a few seconds she felt her mind fading, and her most recent memories were once again proving elusive. She looked around, wondering how she had even ended up back at Hadlow House, hoping that perhaps someone – Anne or Daniel or her parents – might step into view and help her. For a few seconds all the events of her life seemed to somehow blur together, before finally she was able to reassert her own thoughts and she remembered her slow, shivering journey out to the house. Turning to look down at Molly again, she recalled the moment she had held her hands so tightly on the girl's throat. And then, before she had a chance to say anything else, she heard a very familiar creaking sound coming from the doorway.

Sure enough, when she looked out at the hall, she saw that the shapes of moonlight cast across the floor had changed.

"The door is open," she whispered, before looking at Molly again. "The door is open," she said again. "You should go while you still have the chance."

Molly slowly got to her feet. Patience reached out to try to help her, but Molly pulled away.

"I don't blame you," Patience said, before grabbing the girl's hand and forcing her to join her as she walked through into the hallway. She immediately shoved the girl toward the open front door. "You must leave now," she explained, "and never come back. Don't even *look* back, do you understand? Run all the way home to the village and tell your parents what happened, but make sure that they don't come here. And if you can find Anne and Charlotte and Horace, tell them the same thing."

Molly stepped outside, starting to make her way along the path that led toward the gate, and then she turned to Patience again.

"I told you not to do that!" Patience barked at her.

"What about you?" Molly asked. "Aren't you coming too?"

"I cannot."

"But... the door is open."

"That changes nothing," Patience explained. "Nothing in this whole wide world."

"But -"

"There are things you cannot understand at your age," Patience told her. "I certainly did not understand them when I was young, nor did I understand them when I was a good deal older. I understand them now, however, and I just have to... cling onto them for a short while longer. Please, even if it makes no sense to you, run home and keep yourself safe forever. There is nothing here for you, there is nothing here for anyone, I am the last of my bloodline and whatever happens here, whatever has been happening here for so many dreadful years... it ends tonight. Do you understand?"

"I -"

"Go!" Patience screamed.

Clearly startled, Molly turned and ran, racing along the path and then almost clattering into the gate as she struggled to pull it open. Patience watched as the girl disappeared into the distance; she could hear her footsteps crunching through the snow, as more snow fell from the sky, and then finally silence returned.

"I know you're behind me," Patience said, still facing the open door. "I'm not going anywhere. Not this time."

"Why would you go anywhere?" Fanny's

voice asked, as she placed a cold hand on Patience's shoulder. "You're already home."

CHAPTER TWENTY-EIGHT

"AREN'T YOU GOING TO close the door?" Patience asked, still looking out at the moonlit garden.

"Do I need to?"

After pausing for a moment, Patience turned and found herself looking into the dead eyes of Fanny Baxter. A shiver ran through her bones, but she forced herself to remain exactly where she was standing. Something about Fanny's unblinking stare seemed so desperately familiar, as if the intervening years had never passed at all.

"You're not going to climb up the chimney again, are you?" Fanny asked, with the faintest glint of a smile. "I took that as a rather desperate move on your part." She looked Patience up and down for a moment. "Then again," she continued, "I can't imagine you pulling the same trick again, not at your advanced age. But as a sign of good faith, I'm no longer going to keep the front door locked, although I shall close it to keep the heat in."

Patience heard the door bump shut behind her, but she made no move to pull it open again. Already her mind was drifting, and she was having fresh difficulty remembering exactly how she had ended up at Hadlow House again.

"This way, please," Fanny said, gesturing for her to follow as she stepped through into the sitting room. "Three children came to the house today, and I let all three of them leave eventually. The boy might have suffered a little, but that was only to attract some attention. Young Charlotte I allowed to leave unharmed, so that you would see I can be trusted, and it's not my fault if something bad happened to her later. She should have learned to ignore all the instincts she inherited from her father."

Stopping at the chair, the same chair Patience remembering her own father Samuel sitting in many years earlier, she smiled.

"And young Molly left just now, because I had no further use for her. I could have snapped her neck easily, but I did no such thing. Patience, you look so old and so tired. Why don't you sit down?"

"I don't..."

Patience hesitated, before shuffling forward

into the room. She knew there was something she should remember, something important, yet once again her thoughts were blocked by a vast sense of nothingness that seemed to be spreading out through her mind.

"I don't know what I'm doing here," she murmured, as she took a seat in the chair. "I rather fear that I might have forgotten something terribly important."

"Nothing outside of this house is important," Fanny told her, as the fire continued to burn in the hearth. "Not anymore. You will come to understand that in time."

"Where is Daniel?" Patience asked, looking up at her. "I think he would help me to understand a little better. Do you know when he might arrive?"

"There will be time for that later," Fanny said with a benevolent smile. "You have all the time in the world, now that you have finally made the correct choice. I'm so desperately sorry for the time that we lost, Patience, but at least these matters have been put right now, so we shall simply have to make the best out of what we've got. Don't you agree?"

"I..."

Patience hesitated, before turning and looking at the flames in the fireplace. She had a strange memory of having once climbed into that fireplace, and having perhaps clambered up the chimney; she remembered a hand grabbing her ankle as she climbed, yet she was unable to remember how or why such a strange thing might have happened. No matter how hard she tried to think back to that moment, she felt a large force of blankness pushing back and threatening to overcome her thoughts entirely. She tried to fight this sensation for a few more seconds, before letting out a faint sigh as she leaned back a little more in the chair.

"I came to do something," she murmured. "Something important. I just don't quite remember what."

"Then it can't truly have been that important at all, can it?" Fanny replied, placing a hand on her shoulder. "Now why don't you relax for a while? And I'll see if I can rustle up a little something for you."

***

Several hours later, as the bad weather blew more snow against the window, Patience sat in the chair and stared down at the plate of meat on her lap.

"Rabbit," Fanny explained. "Others who have dined here in the house over the years since you left have... not been quite so fortunate with their meals, but I can assure you that what you see on your plate is real. Why would I want to deceive *you*, Patience? There's not a lot of wildlife around the house these days, but occasionally a nice juicy rabbit can be lured closer." She paused. "You should eat."

"I don't remember how," Patience murmured.

"You have a knife and a fork in your hands."

Looking down, Patience saw that Fanny was telling the truth. She furrowed her brow as she tried to remember exactly how these instruments worked, but she felt a little relieved a moment later when Fanny took them from her and began to cut some meat from the rabbit's side.

"Here," Fanny said, packing the meat properly onto the fork before holding it close to her lips. "I must confess, Patience, that I had not understood just how much trouble you would be having with even the most basic of tasks. Why oh why did you not come back to me sooner?"

Patience opened her mouth and allowed Fanny to slip the meat between her lips. She began to chew, and she felt a little proud of herself for even remembering how to perform this simple action. Deep down she understood that something was terribly wrong, but she was so very tired of always fighting to keep her mind running properly.

"That's good," Fanny purred. "Well done, Patience, you're managing to do it. With a little more help, I rather believe that there's some life left in you yet."

"Where's Daniel?" Patience whispered.

"Hush. Forget about Daniel."

"I want to see him," she replied. "Even if it's just one last time, I *have* to see him."

"He's not here," Fanny explained. "There are others who haunt this house, but I'm sorry to say that he is not one of them. Not now. If I could bring him to you, I would."

"I need him," Patience said, as a single tear welled in her right eye, dancing on the lower lid. "You have no idea how much I miss my Daniel."

She looked out toward the hallway, watching the empty space and hoping desperately that her long-lost husband might appear at any moment.

"You're here now," Fanny told her, "and you're safe, and that's all that matters. Why don't you take some time to reminisce about all the good times you enjoyed here in the house? I know things didn't quite end up as they should have done, but before your mother in particular became so troublesome I truly believe that the whole situation was working out."

"You do?"

"Don't you remember?"

"I'm not sure," Patience whispered. "I think so. Perhaps. I remember... working in the kitchen."

"Where I sometimes supervised you," Fanny said, "even if you perhaps didn't quite realize. All of that was ripped away from us, Patience, but now at the end we can get it back. Even if that's not for very long. I must go and check on a few things, but I shall be back shortly and then we can think about getting you upstairs. I've made up a bed for you and I'm sure you're tired."

"You're most kind," Patience murmured, staring ahead at the fire's flickering orange glow as Fanny left the room. "I don't deserve all this fussing, though. I'm sure Daniel will be home soon, and then I can think about trying to get some of my other memories back." She paused again, lost in thought. "I wish I could remember how I ended up here tonight. I was in the village, I believe, and... Horace was talking to me earlier about something. Oh, I've never liked that Horace fellow. If I'm honest, I've always felt that Anne settled a little too easily for him, he's such a lazy thing. She does the best she can, but that's *despite* his so-called help. All he's really provided is dear young Charlotte and..."

Her voice trailed off, and after a moment she looked across the room. In that moment, realizing that she was alone, she took a deep breath and told herself that she was simply going to have to calm down and wait for Daniel.

"You'll be here soon, my darling," she said, as her eyes slipped shut and she began to fall asleep. "I know you will. You always come and make everything alright again. In the end."

CHAPTER TWENTY-NINE

SUDDENLY OPENING HER EYES, Patience realized that she must have briefly fallen asleep. She opened her mouth to call out to Anne, but in that moment she saw snow still falling outside the window and she hesitated for a few seconds; then, slowly, she felt a creeping realization starting to settle in her mind.

"What?" she whispered, looking around the room. "How did I end up..."

Her voice trailed off as she tried to remember how she could possibly have found herself back in Hadlow House. She began to sit up, only to feel her aching bones trying to hold her down. Letting out a faint gasp, she adjusted her position a little in the seat and then she looked over at the open door. The hallway was dark and empty, although she could just about make out the pile of boxes in the old study. Listening to the silence, she began to remember that she had been speaking earlier to the ghost of Fanny Baxter. Looking down at her hands, she saw that they were thin and liver-spotted, and it was only in that instant that she remembered she was so very old.

"I shouldn't be here," she murmured, trying – and failing – once more to get to her feet. Feeling rather agitated, she was already plotting her walk back through the forest. "I must get home."

"You *are* home," a familiar voice said, and she turned to see a figure standing next to the chair. "Don't you think so?"

"Daniel?"

She watched as Daniel stepped around the chair and sat next to her. He was young again, as young as he'd been on their wedding day all those years earlier, and her soul gladdened at the sight of him.

"This place was always in your heart," he pointed out with a calm, comforting smile. Reaching over, he took hold of her hands. "Let's be honest, Patience. Throughout all those years in the village, wasn't a considerable part of your mind still thinking about this house?"

"I'm so glad to see you," she told him. "You're so young, Daniel!"

"I was young when we first met. And so

were you."

"I'm old now."

"You're still the same girl I first met on that dark night," he replied. "The same girl I spent time with on that little bridge over the river."

"I would so dearly like to go there again," she said, with fresh tears in her eyes. "Even if it's for one last time."

"I'm not sure that there'll be time for that."

"Why not?"

"It's a dark and cold night," he pointed out. "I can't believe you made it out here. Fortunately Fanny got this fire going for you, otherwise you might well have frozen to death by now."

"Yes, but -"

Before she could finish, Patience heard the tell-tale sound of a single footstep on the floor of the room above. She looked up at the ceiling, watching as a flickering orange glow from the fireplace caught the wooden boards, but now the house had fallen silent again.

"Do you remember when your mother used to make you clean in here?" Daniel asked.

"She was always so fastidious," Patience replied with a nostalgic smile.

"She was like that in London as well," Daniel continued. "Do you remember in the little house in London, when you'd track soot in from outside and she'd shout at you until you cleaned it up?"

"I used to complain so much," she recalled. "Now I'd give anything for just one more moment back there. It's funny, but after my parents moved us to Cobblefield, I never once set foot anywhere else. I do so wonder what London must be like now, all these years after I left. His Majesty King George was on the throne back then, he'd been brought over from Hanover following the death of Queen Anne. Then his son George took the throne, followed by his own grandson, who now rules as George the Third and..."

Her voice trailed off.

"It's funny," Daniel said, "that you can recall the monarchs of your life in such detail, yet you can scarcely remember what you had for breakfast."

"Some things stick in this foolish old mind of mine better than others," she told him with a wry smile.

"I'm still in there."

"Oh, how could I ever forget you?" she asked, turning to him again. "You are the love of my life, Daniel. I always hoped that your ghost would come to me, I waited and waited, but at least you are here now. You're not some trick, are you? You haven't been conjured up by Fanny Baxter to fool me, have you? I think I would die of horror if that happened."

"I am nothing to do with Fanny Baxter," he

told her, as he began to stroke her hands.

"I believe you," she replied. "Fanny is upstairs, as far as I can tell. She will be down shortly, I'm sure. She mentioned something about preparing a bed for me." She chuckled. "There we go again. I remember that, but I do not remember how I got here." She sat up a little more in the chair, as the fire continued to burn in the hearth. "I hope Anne is not too worried about me," she continued. "That girl has so much on her plate, you know. Her husband is a waste of space. There, I said it. I wouldn't say it to anybody else, Daniel. Only you. You're the only one I trust, and -"

Stopping suddenly, she realized that something was wrong. She stared at him, marveling at the youth of his features, but she was starting to understand that he wasn't a ghost at all. He'd already said several things about her childhood that he couldn't possibly have known, which meant that he wasn't a memory either. For a few seconds she couldn't quite fathom what she was actually seeing, before finally she reached out with one hand and tried to touch his face, only for him to disappear.

"All in my head," she whispered sadly. "Just my way of talking to myself."

Realizing that she was all alone, and that she had been ever since waking up in the chair, she tried again to get to her feet. This time she pushed through the pain, and after a few uncomfortable seconds she was able to stand in the middle of the room.

"Why don't you sit back down?" she heard Daniel's voice saying. "You deserve to rest, Patience."

"Not this time."

"Come on," he continued, touching her hand from behind. "Let's talk. Just you and me, the way we used to back in the old days."

She shook her head.

"Isn't that all you want now?" he asked. "I thought you enjoyed talking to me, Patience."

"More than anyone could ever possibly imagine," she replied, "but I can't let myself slip back into more dreams and fantasies. I've lived that way for decades now, ever since you died. I've been waiting for your ghost to appear to me, fantasizing that you'd come back to me the way other dead people have come back, but now I understand that you're dead and gone. Perhaps you're somewhere else, waiting for me, or perhaps not. Either way, there is nothing to be gained by wishing otherwise."

She heard a creaking sound, as the wind battered the house and more snow fell outside.

"This old place has become the home of evil," she continued, before reaching out and touching the wall. "Through no fault of its own, I might add. Bad things have happened here, and those bad things have stained the house somehow.

It's a good house, I still believe that, but sometimes things just go wrong and one has to recognize that fact."

She ran her hand across the wall, feeling every ripple and fluctuation of its surface as if she was reading its palm, almost as if she was reuniting with an old friend.

"I am so sorry," she said softly, keeping her voice low, "for what must happen. You know that, don't you? For so long I've hated you, but that was unfair. It's what's *inside* you that I hate. It's -"

Before she could finish, she heard another footstep in one of the upstairs rooms, and in that moment she understood that she had to act fast, while her mind was clear and while the opportunity presented itself. She thought for a few seconds, and she was surprised to find that a plan formed fairly quickly in her thoughts. Indeed, she was starting to remember what it had been like to think strongly as a younger woman.

"I will make it as quick and as painless as I can," she said through gritted teeth, before taking one of the old candles and lighting it in the fireplace. "I'm finally ready to do this."

CHAPTER THIRTY

AS SOON AS SHE stepped into the old study, Patience heard the loose floorboard creak behind her in the hallway. She stopped, still holding the burning candle, and she felt a chill against the back of her neck.

"What are you doing in here, Patience?" Fanny asked. "You're supposed to be in the other room. I was about to come and fetch you so that I can put you to bed."

"I have to do something," Patience murmured, already struggling once more to remember. "I can't let myself drift away again."

"There's nothing in here for you," Fanny told her, reaching out and taking hold of her arm from behind. "You should know that. It's cold in here, too. Come back to the room where the fire is burning."

"What about the hole in the chimney?"

"What about it?"

"The room upstairs -"

"I'm not putting you in that room," Fanny replied. "You really mustn't worry about anything. You don't need to think at all." She paused, as if she was waiting for Patience to acquiesce and go with her. "You remind me of your father sometimes," she continued. "You have his stubbornness. I very much hope, however, that you won't persist with any foolish ideas." Another pause. "Why do you have a burning candle?"

"I had to improvise," Patience told her.

"Improvise *what*, exactly?"

Patience wanted to reply, but for a moment she struggled to remember. She looked into the room and saw all the boxes, and the books on the shelves, and she tried to piece together the various ideas that existed as mere fragments in her mind. She knew she had to do something very important, yet somehow that sense of urgency remained unfocused as her thoughts fell apart.

"You were talking to your husband earlier, were you not?" Fanny said. "I'm sure he's waiting to talk to you again."

"No," Patience replied, shaking her head.

"What do you mean by that?"

"I was just imagining him."

"Are you sure he wasn't a ghost?"

"A ghost, or a memory, or a fantasy," Patience said, as she looked down at the boxes. "Sometimes it can be so difficult to tell all those things apart." She stepped forward and pulled the lid from one of the boxes, and she saw that it contained several cubes of tightly-packed powder. At the same time, the wooden lid felt strangely damp in her hand. "You're a ghost, Mrs. Baxter," she continued, "and that I know for certain, at least."

"Come back to the other room, Patience."

"These boxes..."

"They're nothing," Fanny said firmly, sounding a little irritated now. "Those two foolish men from the colonies left them here. I must admit, toying with those idiots gave me something to do in the years I spent waiting for you. They arrived not long after your father's departure. They aren't important, however. Honestly, I do not even remember their names."

"Explosives," Patience whispered as she stared at the packs of powder. "Would they still be good after all these years?"

"You're wasting time and effort," Fanny told her. "Patience, all I want to do is keep the house running, and you are my only surviving employer. I require no salary, and no kindness; I require only somebody to serve. And since you are now so very old, will you not come and sit down so that I can make you comfortable?"

"That would be so easy," Patience said, before flinching as she felt Fanny touching her arm again from behind. "I can't do what's easy."

"Yes, you can," Fanny replied. "And you will. Come now."

"But I was supposed to..."

Patience hesitated, but the idea was already leaving her thoughts. She looked down and saw that already the burning candle was starting to lose its flame. She tried to remember why she was holding the candle in the first place, and she could tell that some urgent need – some sense of determination – had drained from her mind like grains of sand falling through the fingers of a hand.

"This way," Fanny said, pulling Patience out of the room. "It's alright, Patience. It's all going to be perfectly fine."

Turning, Patience told herself that she could perhaps sit back down and think things through. After all, there was no harm in taking some weight off her tired legs, and she desperately wanted to erase the troubles fro her mind. She took a shuffling step forward, allowing Fanny to guide her, and then she stopped as she spotted a familiar figure standing out in the hallway.

"What's wrong?" Fanny asked. "Let's go to the other room."

"Daniel?" Patience whispered.

"There's nobody there," Fanny told her. "Let's go."

"You've waited all this time," Daniel said calmly, still looking so young as he smiled at Patience. "You were right to run from this place, and you were right to come back now. So many people have suffered because of the evil that has been allowed to fester here. You're not long for this world, Patience. Soon you can come and be with me, with the *real* me. First, however, you know what you have to do."

"I want to rest," she told him.

"There's nobody there!" Fanny hissed angrily.

"You've rested enough," Daniel told Patience, "and you get to rest so very soon. But right now, my darling, you have to make sure that nobody else ever suffers at the hands of this evil again."

"Patience," Fanny said, trying to pull her toward the other room, "come and sit down in the warm."

Patience turned to her, and then – pulling away – she stepped back to the boxes and tipped the burning candle onto some of the powdered blocks. She watched as the flames began to spread, but she felt a growing sense of disappointment as she realized that there was no explosion.

"Did you seriously think that anything would happen there?" Fanny asked from the doorway. "All that wretched stuff has been sitting there for a quarter of a century."

Patience saw that the flames were still spreading slowly, but that the only real result was a slow fizzing sound.

"One of those American fools claimed to have developed a special type of explosive," Fanny continued, "but I am sure there must be limits to such matters. Patience, I admire your spirit and your determination, but I had hoped your childish resistance had been left behind a long time ago. If you had just stayed that night, along with your father, I could have been looking after you for so very many years."

Still watching the boxes, Patience saw that the flames appeared to be fizzling out.

"I don't understand," she murmured. "I don't know what to do next."

"You're going to come with me," Fanny told her.

"I'm so sorry, Daniel," Patience continued. "I tried my best, but I'm too late. If I had been brave enough the last time I was out here, I might perhaps have been able to stop her, but I missed my chance." She turned and looked at Fanny. "And now," she added, "she will get exactly what she wants. I can already feel my mind starting to fade again."

"There you are, muttering away again," Fanny said. "You really mustn't let yourself worry about so many things, Patience. Come and sit down, and let all your fears fade away, and I shall do my very best to look after you. Day in and day out, I'll be at your service, the way I always *should* have been at your family's service. Your mother was an ungrateful brute, your father was little better, but I have a strong feeling that finally you're going to be the one who lets me perform my duties. Your blood is my pleasure."

Patience opened her mouth to reply, to tell her that perhaps she might like to relax after all, but at the last second she heard a sudden fizzing and snapping sound. Turning, she looked back at the boxes and saw that the flames had persisted, spreading into some of the other boxes and starting to grow again. She watched for a moment, wondering whether she might be about to succeed, and then – at the last moment – she turned to Fanny again.

"Oh, Fanny," she said, as her mind cleared and she felt as sharp and confident as she had as a twenty-one-year-old girl stepping into Hadlow House for the very first time, "I'm afraid your time as housekeeper here at Hadlow House is very much over." She took a deep breath. "I'm afraid, Mrs. Baxter," she added, "that your services are no longer required."

In that instant, she saw that Fanny finally understood.

Suddenly the boxes exploded, ripping not only the room but one entire side of the house apart, blasting wood and bricks and fabric far and wide, tearing Patience's frail human body almost to atoms and even blowing the roof away. As millions of shards of wood somersaulted through the air, one of the chimney stacks crashed down, bringing several of the bedrooms with it in the process and causing an immense rumbling sound as half the house slammed against the ground and caused the entire clearing to shudder. Debris was blown clear into the forest, and a huge cloud of dust rose up toward the snowy night sky as the initial explosion began to subside.

An ominous creaking sound rang out, and seconds later the vast gaping hole on one side of Hadlow House was closed by the upper section buckling and falling down, ripping away entire walls and casting bricks across the grass. When this was done, silence returned and the cloud of dust was even larger; snow was still falling, and after a few minutes the dust began to clear slightly to reveal the fragmented ruins of what had once been – but was now barely recognizable as – Hadlow House.

EPILOGUE

"IT WOKE ME UP something chronic," Martin Merriford said as he stood in *The Shoemaker* the following morning, supping on a pint of ale. "I thought the heavens themselves had come crashing down."

"I heard there was barely anything left of the place," Jack Keats said, leaning across the bar from the other side. "Just a shell, a few walls and the cellar, and not much else. They found bits of glass and brickwork out between the trees, some of it had even landed in the river."

"And what about Patience?" Martin asked.

"I believe enough was found to make it clear she was there," Jack said cautiously, clearly trying to remain discreet and respectful. "Not a lot, but... I heard there's at least something to bury."

"Apparently no-one has seen the rest of the family since yesterday," Martin continued. "Anne, Patience and even the little girl have just vanished into thin air after the fire."

"There's not much of the old stables left, either," Jack commented. "I'm not sure there's ever been such a dramatic day in all the history of Cobblefield. We're certainly not used to things like this."

"I'll be glad to see the back of Hadlow House," Martin told him. "I hope someone goes and rips down what's left of the place and then salts the ground. Whether you believe in the spirit world or not, you have to admit that something out at that house just wasn't right."

"Let's hope for a quieter time now," Jack murmured, as he looked across the room and saw several other drinkers discussing the latest events with one another. "Lord knows, this place could do with a bit of a rest. And I might be wrong, but I've got a strong feeling that with Hadlow House destroyed – or turned to ruins, at least – we might be in for some much-needed peace."

***

Three men pulled on the branch, twisting and manipulating its length slowly up and through the hole in the ice, until finally they managed to drag the little girl's frozen corpse from its watery grave.

"Set her down here," Marston Ward said, making his way over and watching as Charlotte's body was rolled onto the ground. "Let's get a look at her."

"There's another body down there," one of the other men said, peering at the hole in the ice, "but we can't get to it at the moment. It's wedged under the carriage."

"It can wait until the thaw," Marston replied, crouching down and touching the side of Charlotte's icy, pale face. He brushed some hair away from her features. "Poor little thing," he muttered. "Can't have been more than nine or ten years old, can she? Perhaps a little more. Anyway, it's no way to die. We can only hope it was quick."

"What were they doing, racing around the corner at such speed in the snow?" another man asked. "They were asking for trouble." He turned and looked back past the bridge, and he saw various items that had spilled out from cases that had fallen from the carriage and split open during the crash. A gust of wind blew against his face. "There's no way that anybody had business being out in that snowstorm last night. I can't imagine what might have been so urgent."

"We'll likely never know," Marston told him, before getting to his feet. "Gather up what you can find, although the wind seems to have blown most of it far and wide. We'll put the word out about what happened, and perhaps someone will be able to identify the girl."

He looked down once more at Charlotte's body.

"We'll wait a few days," he added, "and if she's not claimed, we'll have no choice but to bury her in an unmarked grave. Or we can make up a name for her, if people think that'd be more respectful."

"It's a strange old accident, and that's for sure," a man said as he began to pick up some clothes that had landed near the water's edge, having been thrown from the cases just before the carriage had disappeared beneath the ice. "Still, at least the horse survived. He's been taken to get looked after."

Some items from the cases had been blown several hundred meters away. One of those items in particular was the deeds to Hadlow House; this simple page had mostly avoided becoming too wet, and even now was blowing past some gateposts and along the side of the road running into the nearest village. As the wind died down a little, the deeds settled next to a post, but a moment later the wind returned and the deeds were sent blowing about once more, finally coming to a rest next to one of the mile-markers.

The wind ruffled the paper for a moment,

before threatening to blow it away again.

At the last second, however, a black-booted foot stamped down and caught the deeds, holding the piece of paper in place. This was followed by the tip of a silver cane, which kept the deeds secure before a gloved hand reached down and picked up the paper, examining the details that could just about be made out. Despite some damage to the document, the top section could still be read, revealing the name Hadlow House.

Staring at the page in his hands, the one-eyed man seemed focused intently on the barely-legible text. Even as voices called out and Charlotte's body was carried away from the frozen river, the man continued to look at the deeds; his good eye was strikingly blue, while his right eye was missing entirely and no attempt had been made to cover or fill the empty socket at all.

AMY CROSS

NEXT IN THIS SERIES

1837

(THE HAUNTING OF HADLOW HOUSE BOOK 5)

A fresh chapter begins in the history of Hadlow House, as the ruins of the old property are purchased by a new family. Determined to create the perfect countryside retreat, this family sets about restoring Hadlow House to its former glory. But what dark secrets are hiding in this family's past?

Soon after they move in, the new owners start to notice something strange moving through the shadows of their new home. Shocking home truths start bubbling to the surface, and a horrifying tragedy soon rocks every member of the family to their core. Can the family be saved, or is Hadlow House about to claim more victims?

1837 is the fifth book in the *Haunting of Hadlow House* series, which tells the story of one haunted house over the centuries from its construction to the present day. All the lives, all the souls, all the tragedies... and all the ghosts.

Also by Amy Cross

The Haunting of Nelson Street
(The Ghosts of Crowford book 1)

Crowford, a sleepy coastal town in the south of England, might seem like an oasis of calm and tranquility. Beneath the surface, however, dark secrets are waiting to claim fresh victims, and ghostly figures plot revenge.

Having finally decided to leave the hustle of London, Daisy and Richard Johnson buy two houses on Nelson Street, a picturesque street in the center of Crowford. One house is perfect and ready to move into, while the other is a fire-ravaged wreck that needs a lot of work. They figure they have plenty of time to work on the damaged house while Daisy recovers from a traumatic event.

Soon, they discover that the two houses share a common link to the past. Something awful once happened on Nelson Street, something that shook the town to its core.

Also by Amy Cross

The Revenge of the Mercy Belle
(The Ghosts of Crowford book 2)

The year is 1950, and a great tragedy has struck the town of Crowford. Three local men have been killed in a storm, after their fishing boat the Mercy Belle sank. A mysterious fourth man, however, was rescue. Nobody knows who he is, or what he was doing on the Mercy Belle... and the man has lost his memory.

Five years later, messages from the dead warn of impending doom for Crowford. The ghosts of the Mercy Belle's crew demand revenge, and the whole town is being punished. The fourth man still has no memory of his previous existence, but he's married now and living under the named Edward Smith. As Crowford's suffering continues, the locals begin to turn against him.

What really happened on the night the Mercy Belle sank? Did the fourth man cause the tragedy? And will Crowford survive if this man is not sent to meet his fate?

Also by Amy Cross

The Devil, the Witch and the Whore
(The Deal book 1)

"Leave the forest alone. Whatever's out there, just let it be. Don't make it angry."

When a horrific discovery is made at the edge of town, Sheriff James Kopperud realizes the answers he seeks might be waiting beyond in the vast forest. But everybody in the town of Deal knows that there's something out there in the forest, something that should never be disturbed. A deal was made long ago, a deal that was supposed to keep the town safe. And if he insists on investigating the murder of a local girl, James is going to have to break that deal and head out into the wilderness.

Meanwhile, James has no idea that his estranged daughter Ramsey has returned to town. Ramsey is running from something, and she thinks she can find safety in the vast tunnel system that runs beneath the forest. Before long, however, Ramsey finds herself coming face to face with creatures that hide in the shadows. One of these creatures is known as the devil, and another is known as the witch. They're both waiting for the whore to arrive, but for very different reasons. And soon Ramsey is offered a terrible deal, one that could save or destroy the entire town, and maybe even the world.

Also by Amy Cross

The Soul Auction

"I saw a woman on the beach. I watched her face a demon."

Thirty years after her mother's death, Alice Ashcroft is drawn back to the coastal English town of Curridge. Somebody in Curridge has been reviewing Alice's novels online, and in those reviews there have been tantalizing hints at a hidden truth. A truth that seems to be linked to her dead mother.

"Thirty years ago, there was a soul auction."

Once she reaches Curridge, Alice finds strange things happening all around her. Something attacks her car. A figure watches her on the beach at night. And when she tries to find the person who has been reviewing her books, she makes a horrific discovery.

What really happened to Alice's mother thirty years ago? Who was she talking to, just moments before dropping dead on the beach? What caused a huge rockfall that nearly tore a nearby cliff-face in half? And what sinister presence is lurking in the grounds of the local church?

Also by Amy Cross

Darper Danver: The Complete First Series

Five years ago, three friends went to a remote cabin in the woods and tried to contact the spirit of a long-dead soldier. They thought they could control whatever happened next. They were wrong...

Newly released from prison, Cassie Briggs returns to Fort Powell, determined to get her life back on track. Soon, however, she begins to suspect that an ancient evil still lurks in the nearby cabin. Was the mysterious Darper Danver really destroyed all those years ago, or does her spirit still linger, waiting for a chance to return?

As Cassie and her ex-boyfriend Fisher are finally forced to face the truth about what happened in the cabin, they realize that Darper isn't ready to let go of their lives just yet. Meanwhile, a vengeful woman plots revenge for her brother's murder, and a New York ghost writer arrives in town to uncover the truth. Before long, strange carvings begin to appear around town and blood starts to flow once again.

Also by Amy Cross

The Ghost of Molly Holt

"Molly Holt is dead. There's nothing to fear in this house."

When three teenagers set out to explore an abandoned house in the middle of a forest, they think they've found the location where the infamous Molly Holt video was filmed.

They've found much more than that...

Tim doesn't believe in ghosts, but he has a crush on a girl who does. That's why he ends up taking her out to the house, and it's also why he lets her take his only flashlight. But as they explore the house together, Tim and Becky start to realize that something else might be lurking in the shadows.

Something that, ten years ago, suffered unimaginable pain.

Something that won't rest until a terrible wrong has been put right.

Also by Amy Cross

American Coven

He kidnapped three women and held them in his basement. He thought they couldn't fight back. He was wrong...

Snatched from the street near her home, Holly Carter is taken to a rural house and thrown down into a stone basement. She meets two other women who have also been kidnapped, and soon Holly learns about the horrific rituals that take place in the house. Eventually, she's called upstairs to take her place in the ice bath.

As her nightmare continues, however, Holly learns about a mysterious power that exists in the basement, and which the three women might be able to harness. When they finally manage to get through the metal door, however, the women have no idea that their fight for freedom is going to stretch out for more than a decade, or that it will culminate in a final, devastating demonstration of their new-found powers.

AMY CROSS

Also by Amy Cross

The Ash House

Why would anyone ever return to a haunted house?

For Diane Mercer the answer is simple. She's dying of cancer, and she wants to know once and for all whether ghosts are real.

Heading home with her young son, Diane is determined to find out whether the stories are real. After all, everyone else claimed to see and hear strange things in the house over the years. Everyone except Diane had some kind of experience in the house, or in the little ash house in the yard.

As Diane explores the house where she grew up, however, her son is exploring the yard and the forest. And while his mother might be struggling to come to terms with her own impending death, Daniel Mercer is puzzled by fleeting appearances of a strange little girl who seems drawn to the ash house, and by strange, rasping coughs that he keeps hearing at night.

The Ash House is a horror novel about a woman who desperately wants to know what will happen to her when she dies, and about a boy who uncovers the shocking truth about a young girl's murder.

Also by Amy Cross

Haunted

Twenty years ago, the ghost of a dead little girl drove
Sheriff Michael Blaine to his death.

Now, that same ghost is coming for his daughter.

Returning to the small town where she grew up, Alex
Roberts is determined to live a normal, quiet life. For the
residents of Railham, however, she's an unwelcome
reminder of the town's darkest hour.

Twenty years ago, nine-year-old Mo Garvey was found
brutally murdered in a nearby forest. Everyone thinks
that Alex's father was responsible, but if the killer was
brought to justice, why is the ghost of Mo Garvey still
after revenge?

And how far will the real killer go to protect his secret,
when Alex starts getting closer to the truth?

Haunted is a horror novel about a woman who has to
face her past, about a town that would rather forget, and
about a little girl who refuses to let death stand in her
way.

AMY CROSS

Also by Amy Cross

The Curse of Wetherley House

"If you walk through that door, Evil Mary will get you."

When she agrees to visit a supposedly haunted house with an old friend, Rosie assumes she'll encounter nothing more scary than a few creaks and bumps in the night. Even the legend of Evil Mary doesn't put her off. After all, she knows ghosts aren't real. But when Mary makes her first appearance, Rosie realizes she might already be trapped.

For more than a century, Wetherley House has been cursed. A horrific encounter on a remote road in the late 1800's has already caused a chain of misery and pain for all those who live at the house. Wetherley House was abandoned long ago, after a terrible discovery in the basement, something has remained undetected within its room. And even the local children know that Evil Mary waits in the house for anyone foolish enough to walk through the front door.

Before long, Rosie realizes that her entire life has been defined by the spirit of a woman who died in agony. Can she become the first person to escape Evil Mary, or will she fall victim to the same fate as the house's other occupants?

AMY CROSS

Also by Amy Cross

The Ghosts of Hexley Airport

Ten years ago, more than two hundred people died in a horrific plane crash at Hexley Airport.

Today, some say their ghosts still haunt the terminal building.

When she starts her new job at the airport, working a night shift as part of the security team, Casey assumes the stories about the place can't be true. Even when she has a strange encounter in a deserted part of the departure hall, she's certain that ghosts aren't real.

Soon, however, she's forced to face the truth. Not only is there something haunting the airport's buildings and tarmac, but a sinister force is working behind the scenes to replicate the circumstances of the original accident. And as a snowstorm moves in, Hexley Airport looks set to witness yet another disaster.

AMY CROSS

Also by Amy Cross

The Girl Who Never Came Back

Twenty years ago, Charlotte Abernathy vanished while playing near her family's house. Despite a frantic search, no trace of her was found until a year later, when the little girl turned up on the doorstep with no memory of where she'd been.

Today, Charlotte has put her mysterious ordeal behind her, even though she's never learned where she was during that missing year. However, when her eight-year-old niece vanishes in similar circumstances, a fully-grown Charlotte is forced to make a fresh attempt to uncover the truth.

Originally published in 2013, the fully revised and updated version of *The Girl Who Never Came Back* tells the harrowing story of a woman who thought she could forget her past, and of a little girl caught in the tangled web of a dark family secret.

AMY CROSS

AMY CROSS

BOOKS BY AMY CROSS

For more information, visit:

www.amycross.com

AMY CROSS

Printed in Great Britain
by Amazon

25997305R00179